ELMHURST PUBLIC LIBRARY

D0065385

DATE DUE

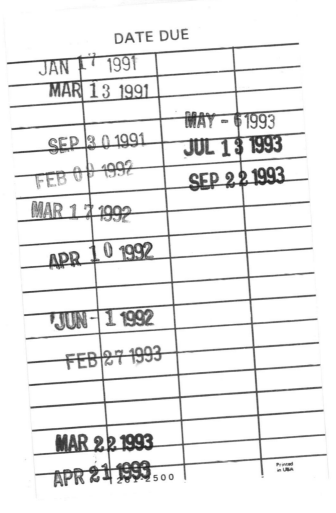

JAN 17 1991		
MAR 13 1991		
	MAY - 6 1993	
SEP 30 1991	JUL 13 1993	
FEB 00 1992	SEP 22 1993	
MAR 17 1992		
APR 10 1992		
JUN - 1 1992		
FEB 27 1993		
MAR 22 1993		
APR 21 1993		Printed in USA

261-2500

A VERY
PAROCHIAL
MURDER

Recent novels by John Wainwright:

Thief of Time
Take Murder...
The Eye of the Beholder
The Venus Fly-Trap
All on a Summer's Day
An Urge for Justice
Cul-de-Sac
The Forest
The Ride
Clouds of Guilt
All Through the Night
Portrait in Shadows
The Tenth Interview
The Forgotten Murders
Blind Brag

F
wainwright
c. 2

A VERY
PAROCHIAL
MURDER

John Wainwright

St. Martin's Press
New York

A VERY PAROCHIAL MURDER. Copyright © 1988 by John & Avis
Wainwright. All rights reserved. Printed in the United States
of America. No part of this book may be used or reproduced
in any manner whatsoever without written permission
except in the case of brief quotations embodied in critical
articles or reviews. For information, address St. Martin's
Press, 175 Fifth Avenue, New York, N.Y. 10010.

Library of Congress Cataloging-in-Publication Data

Wainwright, John William.
    A very parochial murder / John Wainwright.
        p.   cm.
    ISBN 0-312-02309-X
    I. Title.
PR6073.A354V4   1988
823'.914—dc19   88-17668
                                                    CIP

First published in Great Britain by Macmillan London
Limited.

First U.S. Edition

10 9 8 7 6 5 4 3 2 1

A VERY
PAROCHIAL
MURDER

ELMHURST PUBLIC LIBRARY
ELMHURST, IL 60126

1

April was three days old. The nights still held that hint of frost, pavement-strolling coppers had not yet abandoned their greatcoats during the darkness hours and, on this morning, the pewter-coloured sea reflected a pale sun from a cloudless sky and a steady breeze from the west kept all but the joggers and dog-walkers from the promenade.

A couple more months and the holidaymakers would be taking ritualistic before-breakfast strolls in the summer warmth. Later in the day, deck-chairs and picnic-tables would be scattered around the green. The shelters along Rock Walk would house the less robust visitors. Rogate-on-Sands would be enjoying the first flush of its annual 'season'.

But on this particular April day the flags atop the poles erected in the grounds of the seafront hotels flew stiff and steadily and what few guests the hotels were catering for sat in comfort behind the double-glazing of sun-lounges.

Muriel Jackson was not a visitor. She had been born at Rogate-on-Sands; her parents had been the proprietors of a tiny hotel a few streets away from the front; she'd been educated at the local school and, after leaving school, had served behind the counter of a multiple store. In her late teens she'd met her husband at one of the local hops; they'd been married in the seafront parish church and, seven years ago, her father had been lowered into a grave in the yard of the church. Less than a year ago her widowed mother had followed him.

5

An echo of the emotional turmoil surrounding her mother's death swept over her as she arranged fresh daffodils. Sadness, anger and frustration swirled in a crazy mix and pricked the back of her eyes. The death had been so sudden, so violent, so futile.

It had been so . . .

She shook her head in an attempt to clear her mind of tumbling hurtful memories and straightened from the grave. The wind from the sea stung her face, but the redbrick surround of the churchyard shielded the grave and, hopefully, the blooms would last until the same time next week.

She walked the flagged path, past other headstones and smaller plots where cremation had done away with the need for size. The grass between the graves had already had its first crop of summer, and the scent of newly mown turf sweetened the air. She pushed open the heavy door of the church. Inside, she lowered herself on to the hard surface of one of the rear pews, linked her fingers, lowered her head and prayed.

It was a strange prayer, but one she offered every week. She sought forgiveness – but was unsure of what personal sin she had committed. She mentally spoke to her Maker as she'd once spoken to her father; when, as a child, she'd misbehaved herself in some small way and her father had been disappointed rather than disapproving; when she'd known she'd let him down, albeit only a little, and childlike she'd wished she hadn't and, in effect, had pleaded that both clock and calendar be reversed and, magically, that which had caused displeasure might, on the rerun, not be committed.

She was a grown woman. She wasn't a fool. She knew the impossibility of what she asked. But such was her everlasting distress that adult logic was thrown aside. She sought a miracle, knowing that no miracle was possible.

6

2

'Just rumours?' The Chief Constable looked mildly worried as he asked the question.

'That's all they are at the moment, sir.'

Lyle had driven to force headquarters directly from his home. His appointment with the chief had been for 10 a.m. – the first appointment of the day – but the Rogate-on-Sands detective chief inspector had been deliberately early: 9.30 a.m. had seen him sitting in the waiting-room adjacent to the chief's office. Chief constables were notorious fellows for flying off at tangents; skipping one meeting in order to attend another and, to them, more important meeting. Lyle had been waiting when the chief had arrived.

And now, having dropped his bombshell, Lyle waited for top-office reaction.

'Missing from Home?' mused the chief. It was not so much a question as an opening gambit to a discussion which might lead to a decision.

'For three weeks,' said Lyle. 'Three weeks last Friday, to be precise. Treated as such – as an adult Missing from Home – and nothing more.'

'But you think he's been murdered?'

'I think it is a possibility.' Lyle chose his words very carefully. 'We know the man. We know his lifestyle – if you can call it that. There's no logical *reason* for him to go missing.'

'Not "seeking his fortune"?' smiled the Chief Constable.

'That's the last thing he'd do. He's a damn nuisance – has been for years – but he has sense enough to value a roof over his head.'

'And if the rest of your information is correct?' This question was not accompanied by a smile.

'We have trouble,' said Lyle solemnly.

'Something of an understatement, surely?'

'That's why I'm here, sir.'

'To pass the baby?'

'No, sir.' Lyle was wise enough to know his mettle was being quietly tested. He said; 'I can handle things, but I need somebody to guard my back.'

'Superintendent Crosby?' suggested the chief mildly.

'Not Superintendent Crosby.' Lyle kept all expression from his voice.

'I'm inclined to agree, Chief Inspector.' sighed the Chief Constable. He paused, then said: 'Strictly within the confines of this office, Lyle. Your unofficial appraisal and what *you* think should be done.'

While Lyle talked, the Chief Constable seemed to focus his eyes upon the glass-fronted cabinet which half-filled one wall of the office. It was a large cabinet. One shelf was filled with the standard law-books necessary in order to enforce a Criminal Law which seemed to grow more complex each week. The other shelves sported various trophies either won or temporarily held by the force: shields for cricket and rugby, cups for first-aid and life-saving prowess, platters for achievement at darts, at bowls, at boxing. It was quite an impressive display and worth looking at – had the Chief Constable *been* looking.

Lyle said: 'We can do without the Jimmy Doyles of this world. That's my first reaction. Three Saturday nights running, and we haven't had trouble of some sort in which he was involved. I can't remember when *that* happened last. If he's merely upped sticks and left the district, good luck to him. That's fine by me. If, on the other hand, rumour is more than mere rumour, that's another thing entirely. Dead, I couldn't care less. *Murdered*, I *have* to care.' He hesitated, before adding: 'Not because *he's* been murdered

8

– by rights he should be inside one of Her Majesty's prisons, serving a life sentence – but because he's *been* murdered, and I happen to take my job very seriously.'

'Mary Sutcliffe?' The Chief Constable spoke the name gently, while still staring at the contents of the cabinet.

Before Lyle could reply the telephone on the chief's desk shrilled a startling interruption. The Chief Constable brought his eyes back into focus, frowned quick annoyance and picked up the receiver. His conversation to his secretary was curt, almost to the point of rudeness.

'Yes? . . . At the moment that's not possible. . . . I don't give a damn how insistent he is. Give him my apologies and tell him I'll give him a ring when I'm free. . . . Good God, woman! You're employed as *my* secretary. Explain that to him – if it *needs* explaining – and, with my compliments, tell him I have a force to run, and that's exactly what I'm doing. And, until further notice, I want no more calls passed through to this office.'

He replaced the receiver, blew out his cheeks, then said: 'Chief Inspector, *never* envy this chair. Small men, with tin-pot authority – members of the Police Committee – claim the right to order chief constables around to suit their own convenience.'

Lyle smiled his sympathy, then said: 'About Doyle?'

'Let me get the problem into perspective,' said the chief bluntly. 'You've had the tip-off that Doyle's been murdered?'

'Yes, sir.'

'The tip-off came from a man you tend to believe, but a man you think is more than a little frightened?'

'That's about the strength of it, sir.'

'*He* was told by a woman known to be something of a gossip?'

Lyle nodded.

'*She* claims to have been told by a woman who – to put it bluntly – at this moment hasn't both oars in the water?'

'Put that way—'

'Isn't that the way it *is*?'

'Yes sir,' sighed Lyle.

'And *she*,' concluded the chief, 'says she was told by the murderer?'

'The man who just rang.' Lyle gave a single nod towards the telephone. 'I don't want to manufacture bullets for people like *him*.'

'No more do I,' growled the chief. 'But – unlike him – we're coppers, Lyle. Our job is to paddle barbed-wire canoes up crocodile-infested creeks.'

'It's a living,' said Lyle mildly.

'Does it,' asked the chief, 'involve listening to hearsay, to gossip, to tittle-tattle?'

'It involves gut feelings, sir.'

There was the sagacity of the lifetime's experience in the chief's slow nod of agreement.

'I think it equally likely that Doyle *has* been murdered, sir,' said Lyle. 'I think it equally likely we already know the name of his murderer.'

'Gut feelings?'

'Yes, sir.'

The Chief Constable was old-fashioned enough to use a cigarette-case. He chose a cigarette, then snapped the case shut without offering it to Lyle. He tapped the cigarette on to the face of the case as he spoke.

'A personal opinion, Chief Inspector. Would he crack under interview?'

'No, sir.' There was absolute certainty in the reply.

'Evidence?'

'None, so far.'

The chief fished a throwaway lighter from his pocket, placed the cigarette between his lips and snapped the lighter into flame.

He exhaled before he said: 'That's it, then. Go back to Rogate-on-Sands. *Find* evidence . . . if there is any. Keep your counsel, and don't scare him away. Give him rope. Hope he'll hang himself.'

'*You* had to know,' said Lyle.

'Of course . . . if only to guard *your* back.'

Lyle ignored the mild gibe and said: 'If it *is* murder, I need one more man to know.'

'Really?' The chief cocked an eyebrow.

'I can't be everywhere. I can't make things *too* obvious. I also need to sleep.'

'Crosby?' The suggestion was made with a mischievous smile as the chief raised the cigarette to his lips.

'Faber,' said Lyle.

'Faber? Isn't he a—'

'A detective inspector. Not run-of-the-mill.'

'Superintendent Crosby *has* mentioned him,' said the chief.

'I'd like Faber alongside me, sir.'

'If it *does* end up as murder,' said the Chief Constable, 'bring Faber into things. And keep *me* informed.'

'Of course.'

'I'll guard your back, Chief Inspector.' The Chief Constable was very serious. 'Just one more thing, before you go.'

'Yes, sir?'

'Objectivity isn't easy. Don't forget that.'

'No, sir.'

3

Little more than an hour later Lyle was speaking to Detective Sergeant Robert Jackson. Lyle was a chief inspector in the CID but, as a man, he knew his job well enough not to indulge in rank-pulling. Jackson could carry his corner, and had done since he'd arrived at Rogate-on-Sands as a young copper almost twelve years before. He'd moved from the pavements to CID having proved himself as CID-Aide and, thereafter, promotion had just been a matter of time.

'Your pigeon, Bob.' Lyle raised the plastic beaker of scalding-hot tea to his lips and sipped, gingerly. 'Last known whereabouts. The general picture and pattern of his life. The usual thing.'

'We *know* the pattern of his life.'

'Quite. But – y'know – missing for three weeks. More. Pending proof to the contrary, we have to accept certain possibilities.'

'That he won't come back,' grumbled Jackson. 'And *that* wouldn't break *my* heart.'

'Nor mine,' smiled Lyle. 'Just that he *could* come back . . . should he get the urge.'

'You think he might be dead?' Jackson sounded surprised.

'I don't know.'

'Does it worry you?'

'Not much.' Lyle moved a shoulder. 'If he's had an accident – if he's gone the way of his old man – that's *it*. I like things to be tidy . . . no more than that.'

They were in the canteen of Rogate-on-Sands Divisional Headquarters, a modern building whose interior still carried the faint smell of fresh paint. The Formica tops of the canteen tables had yet to be brown-stained by lighted cigarettes left smouldering. The covers of the strip-lighting were not yet spotted with dead flies. The vending machine in one corner was still functioning. Near the ceiling an angled television set showed a moving image to those who cared to watch, but the volume of the sound was permanently quietened sufficiently to allow those who wanted to talk to carry on a normal conversation without distraction.

Lyle and Jackson were seated at one of the tables.

Jackson flipped through the slim file Lyle had handed to him and mused: 'Friday night. The weekly disco on the pier.'

'Last seen there.' Lyle tried the tea again and, this time, it had cooled slightly and he was able to drink. 'Since then, nothing.'

Jackson was glancing through the few reports in the folder. He raised his plastic beaker and tasted black coffee.

'His pals have been seen.'

'Some.' Lyle tasted rapidly cooling tea. 'Those at the disco on that night.'

'Pissed of course,' Jackson's lip curled.

'What else?'

'Dammit!' Jackson slapped the file closed. 'I've better things to do, Chief Inspector. If the bastard *isn't* found—'

'No loss.' Lyle ended the sentence for him, then added: 'Nevertheless. . . .'

There was a moment or two of silence. Jackson took cigarettes from the pocket of his jacket and held the opened packet towards Lyle. Lyle took a cigarette, then leaned towards a nearby table for one of the cheap, tin ashtrays.

When they were smoking, Lyle repeated: 'We have to accept certain possibilities, Bob.'

Jackson looked unconvinced.

'A few enquiries,' insisted Lyle. 'Go over the ground again. Christen Number One Incident Centre.'

'All mod cons,' murmured Jackson.

'Of course.' Lyle smiled. 'A new-fangled card-index system waiting to be used. There's even a computer-point. . . .'

'For an adult Missing from Home?'

'If it becomes necessary.'

'There's more to this than meets the eye,' said Jackson slowly. Suspiciously.

'Not really.' Lyle's look of innocence was quite perfect.

They smoked and sipped in silence for a few moments. Lyle had spent the morning driving to and from Force Headquarters. Jackson had been catching up with the ever-present paperwork: reading crime files and reports; verifying that the various legal points necessary for a successful prosecution had been dealt with.

Both were conscientious CID men. Both had long learned that the job held no glamour; that boredom far outweighed the minor excitements. Lyle had called at Jackson's office, handed him the Missing from Home papers and suggested that they discuss things on the neutral ground of the DHQ canteen, while at the same time easing their respective burdens with 'elevenses'.

Jackson said: 'He could have hoofed it out of our territory.'

'He could,' agreed Lyle. 'His mother doesn't think so.'

'His mother hates the sight of him.'

'True . . . but she's sure he'd have let her know.'

'Why the hell *should* he? He's not that sort.'

'He's *every* bloody sort. *Any* bloody sort.' Lyle took a deep breath. 'Look – for me – he need *never* come back . . . good riddance. Let's just say the thing smells slightly. Let's call it a personal indulgence. I'd like to know where he is.'

'Three weeks.' Jackson wasn't arguing. He was merely hinting at a personal opinion. 'An eighteen-year-old. An "adult". A young tearaway, with more booze and disorderly convictions to his name than a dog has fleas. And because he hasn't been home for three weeks *we* get hot around the collar.'

'Silly,' agreed Lyle mildly.

'Because it's Jimmy Doyle?'

'Because it's Jimmy Doyle.' Lyle nodded. 'Because characters like Jimmy Doyle get themselves into trouble . . . all the time. Because he's too dumb to keep out of trouble, and *we* should have known by now. Somebody should have been

14

screaming for his Previous Convictions. Because, wherever he is, he's not sleeping under a hedge or curling up for the night in some barn somewhere. Not this weather. His kind don't go in for the "knights of the road" caper. If it's at all possible, I want to know where he is, Bob. That's the job I'm giving you.'

4

Few beat constables patrolled the prom in bad weather. Especially out of season. It wasn't necessary. The few cafés and ice-cream parlours were closed and shuttered. Rock Walk separated the promenade proper from the coast-road traffic and the seafront hotels and shops, and there was damn-all on Rock Walk of interest to petty thieves. Therefore, few constables patrolled the prom.

Nevertheless, Police Constable 417 Gul always patrolled at least *part* of the promenade whenever he drew West Two Beat. Gul – Jan Gul – was an English citizen. He'd been born in Bradford twenty-five years previously. He was, therefore, English – even Yorkshire, and nobody can be more 'English' than *that* – but of pure Pathan parentage.

Gul was, arguably, the most hard-working and con-scientious beat copper in the whole of Rogate-on-Sands Division. Perhaps in the whole force.

And yet . . .

Nobody had to tell Gul about colour discrimination. Nobody had to draw *him* diagrams. Therefore, perhaps because of his dusky hue, Police Constable Gul never cut corners. He never left the knob of lock-up property untried or the windows unchecked for possible entry. He never short-cut his way around any beat in order to gain

15

a few snatched minutes of shelter from lousy weather. The others did, but Gul *didn't*.

It wasn't that Gul was either proud or ashamed of the colour of his skin. It was the colour of his skin – full stop. *He* didn't need suntan lotion. He was, moreover, English. He was a *Yorkshireman*, for God's sake. He suffered no secret yen to visit either India or Afghanistan; from what he'd seen on the box they were both grubby fly-infested corners of the globe. His hairstyle was short-back-and-sides. He was clean-shaven. His religion – whenever his thoughts touched upon religion – was mild Church of England, with a leaning towards Methodism, if only because Pam, his wife, claimed to be Methodist – and, anyway, chapel hymns had more guts and were more tuneful than some of the miserable dirges warbled by the orthodox crowd.

Nevertheless, he was coloured.

His complaint – if, in fact he *had* a complaint – was that some of his colleagues – *most* of his colleagues – couldn't quite accept him for *exactly* what he was. A fellow-copper. That, and nothing more. Not a novelty. Not a blasted mascot. And, for sure, not a clown wearing police uniform who secretly approved of coloured yobs running wild at periodic race riots in some of the big cities. Not even some clandestine banner-waver in the everlasting rights-of-ethnic-minorities craziness.

As Gul viewed things, everybody was part of some 'minority'. Everybody! Fewer people had blue eyes than *didn't* have blue eyes. Fewer people played golf than *didn't* play golf. Fewer women wore stockings than wore tights. If official statistics were to be believed, the number of women in the United Kingdom outnumbered the men.

Everybody was part of some damn 'minority'.

Gul would have claimed that that was part of his personal logic. But the logic seemed to fall short. Emotion, too, squeezed into things. An emotion which, while rarely unfriendly, seemed to preclude him from that hell-or-high-water closeness enjoyed by some coppers for, and by, certain of their colleagues.

Gul sighed, wiped such thoughts from his mind, bent his head against the steady push of the wind and continued his patrol of the near-deserted promenade.

A stranger touched his arm, and said: 'Excuse me, Constable.'

'Eh?'

The stranger pointed. 'Over there. By the water's edge.'

Gul turned and squinted into the wind.

The stranger said: 'He seems to have fainted.' Then added: 'Or something.'

That 'Or something' carried a breathless innuendo.

Gul took notice of the stranger for the first time. He saw a middle-aged man, dressed for the weather and apparently out bird-watching. Amateur ornithology was a popular hobby in the town; the dippers and waders gave gentle pleasure to those interested in such things.

Gul said: 'Can I borrow your binoculars, please?'

The stranger unlooped the binoculars from the neck and handed them to Gul. Gul peered through them, adjusted them slightly but did not give them back. Somebody might want more details from this stranger and, while Gul had the binoculars, the stranger would stay.

Gul used his walkie-talkie.

'Four-one-seven to Control.'

'Control to Four-one-seven. Go ahead.'

'I'm on West Two.' Gul glanced along the sweep of the prom. 'About two hundred yards south of the pier head. There's something at the water's edge. It looks like a man. He may have fainted. He may be our Missing from Home.'

'Are you with him, Four-one-seven?'

'No. I'm on the prom.'

'Stay there, Four-one-seven. I'll have back-up with you as soon as possible.'

17

5

Jimmy Doyle. Full style and title: James Arnold Simon Doyle . . . deceased. He was no longer Missing from Home. He'd 'arrived' home. He was now (to use an equally well-worn police term) Life Extinct. Very much Life Extinct! His tongue protruded. His face was bloated. The fish had been at him. The cord around his neck still bit deep into the flesh, and his features had been made foul and mottled by the action of the sea-water.

Doyle was not merely dead. Doyle had been murdered.

Since Gul had blown the start-whistle things had moved at a brisk pace. The tide had been on the turn, and only a limited amount of time was available in which to scour the damp sands before the oncoming waves reached the base of the prom.

'Not that we'll find anything,' observed Lyle sourly. 'The current seems to have rolled him ashore. It's a million to one against him having been strangled near *here*.'

'A boat, from the end of the pier?' suggested Jackson. 'Into deep water – comparatively deep water – and the tides have done the rest?'

'Three weeks?' grunted Lyle.

Other than the pawmarks of a pair of dogs out for a lonely frolic, only the footprints of policemen interrupted the sweep of the beach within more than fifty yards of the body. The weather was on the side of law-enforcement. A warmer day or a time of year when holidaymakers were more plentiful, and the task would have been much more difficult. A hundred dead ends would have had to be followed.

18

'It depends when,' said Jackson.

'What?' Lyle raised a questioning eyebrow.

'When he was strangled.' Jackson expounded his theory.

'The pathologist should tell us,' growled Lyle. 'Meanwhile – subject to his findings – we assume on the night he went missing.'

'In that case, I agree. Not around here.'

Lyle waited.

Jackson continued: 'Three weeks. From the end of the pier – even from a boat taken some distance out – he'd have been ashore before now.'

'A reasonable assumption,' agreed Lyle.

They were standing on the promenade, staring with half-closed eyes into the wind and watching the other coppers moving about the beach. The Poor Bloody Infantry and the self-styled 'experts'. The photographers recording the scene. The coppers wearing gumboots, wading into the shallow tide and preparing the corpse for the heavy canvas-and-rubber body-bag. The line of men and women – uniformed and CID – walking slowly across the still-uncovered sand, heads bent and staring at their moving feet, as if in deep thought.

'Going through the motions,' sighed Lyle.

'They won't find anything,' agreed Jackson.

'Of course they won't find anything.' Lyle glanced across at the gathering crowd of spectators already lining the rails of the prom. He said: 'The show, Sergeant, is for *their* benefit. They pay our wages. They like to see value for money.'

'They'll sympathise with him, of course,' observed Jackson.

'Who?'

'The crowd. Those who don't know him or know what he was like. He's been murdered, therefore all past sins are forgiven.'

'Not by me,' said Lyle grimly.

'Not by anybody who really *knew* him.'

'Is this your first?' asked Lyle softly.

'Eh?' Jackson jerked his attention from where the uniformed coppers were bundling the corpse into the unzipped body-bag.

'Your first murder?'

'Oh – er – yes.' A humourless smile flickered for a moment across Jackson's lips. 'They don't come every day.'

'Better than an old lady,' murmured Lyle.

Jackson frowned non-understanding.

'Him.' Lyle jerked his head. 'Better Doyle than some harmless old lady.'

'Much better.' It was a grim and low-spoken agreement.

'You weren't on that one, of course.'

'No.'

The crowd of onlookers thickened by the minute. Rubber-neckers fascinated by the externals of violent death. Two motor-patrol men and a uniformed sergeant kept them beyond listening distance of Lyle and Jackson and prevented them from descending the steps to the sand in order to gape ghoulishly at the business of retrieving a murdered man from the sea.

Lyle pursed his lips, and said: 'Some of the sods would still rob graves.'

'They'd spew their hearts out.'

'That they would,' agreed Lyle. In a slightly sadder tone he added: 'Not a nice way to die . . . even for Doyle.'

'What?' Mild annoyance touched Jackson's expression. As if, quite suddenly, the gawping crowds disgusted him beyond words. He seemed angry and ready only for brooding silence.

'Strangulation,' continued Lyle. '*Not* a nice way to die.'

'I wouldn't know.'

'At a guess, it takes time. Even a *long* time.'

'Nor do I damn well care.'

'Quite.' Lyle nodded solemn approval. 'Objectivity, Bob. Don't let the fact that the bastard's been murdered interfere with conduct of the inquiry.'

20

A man in his late twenties ended a whispered conversation with the uniformed sergeant and was allowed to approach Lyle and Jackson. He wore the near-regulation 'uniform' of the provincial reporter. Belted mac, corduroy trousers and Hush Puppy shoes. He smiled a dubious greeting at Lyle before he spoke.

'Can you tell me anything, Chief Inspector?'

'Doyle.' Lyle was friendly enough. He knew the man; knew confidences would be kept and journalistic imagination not be allowed to take over. 'Jimmy Doyle. He seems to have been strangled, then dumped overboard.'

'Hopwood Close?' The reporter scribbled in his notebook as he asked the question.

'That's the one,' verified Lyle. 'That's about all we can tell you at present.'

'Thanks.'

'Keep it quiet until we've notified next of kin.'

'Of course.' The reporter looked up, then asked: 'It's early days, but – y'know – any leads? Off the record, of course.'

'Nothing more than educated guesses. Given a modicum of luck, we'll find enough evidence.'

'Any hope of a hint?' The question had to be asked, but the reporter didn't expect an answer.

'The murderer knows.' Lyle chuckled gently. 'Eventually *you'll* know.'

6

'The Doyles of Kilkenny, me bucko. The purest Irish blood ever to flow through a man's veins.'

That had been the oft-shouted boast of James Doyle

senior. He'd bawled it in saloon bars and drinking-dens from Liverpool all the way north to Carlisle. It had become his battle-cry – his war-whoop – immediately prior to smashing furniture and glasses and soiling the interior of some boozing-dump with the spilling of that precious blood.

His passing had been as violent and even more spectacular than that of his son.

The 'travelling man', making his way north to the horse-fairs of the North-East, had known even more about bar-room brawling than Doyle. Five minutes, a broken jaw and two broken ribs later, Doyle had realised he'd met his match.

Some said his injured pride had caused Doyle senior to die of a broken heart. The pathologist had disagreed. At the coroner's inquest the pathologist had insisted that James Doyle senior had died from a ruptured spleen.

It had been most unsatisfactory – especially since the 'travelling man' had strolled away from the scene of the carnage before the police had arrived, and had never been seen again.

Kate Doyle had taken the news of her husband's death with stoical indifference. She'd identified the body, given brief evidence, then caught a bus back to Rogate-on-Sands.

That had been all of seven years ago, and now, as she waited for verification of the death of her younger son, her mood was unchanged.

'I should sit down, Mrs Doyle,' suggested the police-woman gently.

'Two of you.' Kate Doyle's tone was both sad and wise.

'Please, Mrs Doyle, sit down.'

'It doesn't take *two* to tell me he's still alive.'

'Please.' The policewoman moved a hand towards a cheap armchair.

'Why?'

'It might be best.' Jackson's voice was gentle.

22

'You've found him, have you?' Kate Doyle dutifully lowered herself on to the armchair. She looked at the detective sergeant, then added: '*You'll* not be sorry.'

'If there's anything we can . . .'

'He's dead, isn't he?'

'I'm afraid so.'

'We're sorry,' added the policewoman.

'And there's a lie, if ever there was one,' said Kate Doyle calmly. 'He's given the police far too much trouble for *them* to be sorry.'

She pronounced the word 'police' as if it was spelled 'powliss'. There was no anger. No accusation. Merely a statement of the truth as she knew it to be.

In a faraway voice, she continued: 'He was like his father, y'know. Too much like his father. He was bad luck to everybody – himself included.'

Jackson moistened his lips, then said: 'He was murdered, Mrs Doyle.'

'Ay.' In some odd way it seemed to be a gesture of gentle agreement. 'It's no more than he deserved. The badness *he's* done – wouldn't you say?'

'We really *are* sorry, Mrs Doyle,' insisted the policewoman. 'We're sorry to have to break the news. We're sorry for *you*.'

'My lovely. . . .' For a moment a film of infinite sadness clouded the older woman's eyes. 'You're not married – no, of course you're not - so you won't know the truth of it. Men! They give you pain, my lovely. Pain . . . that's *all* they give you. His father. Holy mother of God! The times *he* marked me. The times I put make-up on thick enough to make me look a tart. To cover the bruises. To keep the neighbours from knowing he'd fisted me in the face. And Jimmy. Jimmy was as bad as his father. He wanted something. Money. Money for fags. Money for booze. Money for *anything*. If he didn't get it, first time of asking, he was there. Like his father. *Worse* than his father.' Her words

23

were a plea to be understood. 'I'll not weep for Jimmy, my lovely. I didn't weep for his father. I won't weep for *him*.'

'If we *can* help in any way.'

The policewoman's face was pale with controlled emotion. No outrage. No disgust. Only a strange eagerness – woman to woman – to share a hurt.

Jackson said: 'We'll let Michael know.'

'Michael.' She spoke the word softly. It was accompanied by a smile, a sad but happy smile. 'He'll come, now. Now Jimmy isn't here.'

'Michael can identify the body.'

'A cup of tea?' suggested the policewoman.

'Have you any brandy in the house?' added Jackson.

'Medicinal.' Again, her lips curved in a quick and slightly bitter smile. 'Jimmy didn't know. Jimmy didn't know *everything*.' She paused; then, more briskly, said: 'We'll enjoy a cup of tea, with a nip of brandy. Let's toast him on his way. Let's hope the good Lord can forgive easier than his poor old mother.'

7

The Detective Chief Superintendent was Head of CID; therefore, because a murder had been committed he was required to visit Rogate-on-Sands and ginger things up a bit. That (as he saw it) was his job. Lighting a few touch-papers. Firing a few rockets. *That* . . . not detecting crime. The underlings detected crime. *He* made sure they worked their balls off.

Not that he wanted to become too involved. Not with a run-of-the-mill, ten-a-penny, fiddling little killing. Two

24

more years to a nice steady pension, then he could spend *all* his time rose-growing.

He'd been lucky to make detective chief superintendent – and he knew it. A bank robbery when the getaway car had crashed within half a mile of take-off. A murder where the victim had lived long enough to whisper the name of his killer. An attempted insurance fraud where the arsonist had had to be rescued from the fire of his own making. Those had been the highlights of his career. The rungs of the ladder. Luck, my old son. Luck, plus the knack of squirming from under the weight of responsibility when things screwed themselves up.

'As few cock-ups as possible, Lyle,' he grunted.

'None . . . if possible,' promised Lyle.

'What about manpower?'

'It's out of season, and very few of the members of the division have yet started *their* holidays.'

Obviously the Chief Constable had not mentioned his conversation to the Head of CID. That was OK, even if it left Lyle holding a baby which could become very messy.

'Plenty of buckshee shoe-leather, eh?' The DCS grinned.

'We'll get by.'

'Rob Peter to pay Paul,' advised the DCS. 'Sod the old ladies. Let 'em find their own way across busy streets, eh?'

'More or less.'

'Good.' The DCS eyed Lyle's new office. 'They've done you proud, Chief Inspector.'

'It makes a change.'

'Very stylish. Very stylish indeed.'

'It's an improvement.' Lyle was noncommittal. He wanted this self-opinionated clown from under his feet as soon as possible.

'Room enough to stretch your legs, what?'

'When I have time to *be* here.'

'Eh? Oh . . . quite.' The DCS frowned in order to add

25

weight to solemn advice. 'Keep your finger firmly on the button, Lyle. A murder inquiry . . . no passengers. And no would-be high-flyers trying to make everybody else look like so many prize prats.'

'This isn't my first murder inquiry, sir,' said Lyle pointedly.

'No. No . . . of course it isn't. You've a fine record. You wouldn't be where you are if you hadn't.'

'And, of course,' added Lyle innocently, 'there's always *your* experience to fall back on.'

'Eh?'

'If things get knotted up.'

'Oh!' For a moment the DCS looked quite startled, then he wiped the expression from his face and said: 'Of course. That's what I'm there for.'

'I'll remember that, sir.'

'But as you say . . .' The DCS waved a vaguely dismissive hand. 'You've had experience of murder inquiries, Lyle. Ask the right people the right questions. That's all it boils down to. This . . . what's his name?'

'Doyle. Jimmy Doyle.'

'Somebody must have *wanted* to murder him.'

'Of course.'

'Somebody must have hated his guts.'

'Lots of people.'

'That's it, then. No problem. Just sling some weight around, eh?'

'Put that way,' said Lyle flatly.

'Nevertheless. . . .' The DCS hoisted himself from the chair and prepared to leave. 'Any snags – any hiccups – give me a ring.'

'I'll do that, sir.'

8

Michael Doyle handled the power-saw as if it was a Woolworths toy. He swung it effortlessly in one hand as he crossed the lawn to ask a favour of his boss.

Jimmy Doyle's elder brother was a massive person. He topped the six-foot mark by at least two inches. His breadth of shoulder seemed to make any ordinary doorway inadequate. The muscular arms protruding from the short sleeves of the T-shirt were Rambo-like, but real. There was power there. Power in his huge frame, power in the easy length of his stride.

'Jimmy's dead.'

He spoke to the foreman in charge of the landscape-gardening gang of which he was a part. His voice belied his physical stature. It was a gentle voice – almost a shy voice – and, as always, it seemed to carry an overtone of apology.

The gang boss had watched Jackson and the police-woman speak with Michael Doyle. He'd seen Doyle give a solemn nod of understanding and now he knew the reason for the visit.

The foreman said: 'I'm sorry.'

'I'm not.'

'Do you want the rest of the day off?' asked the foreman.

'I'd like to check with the old lady. See she doesn't need anything.'

'Tell your mother I'm sorry,' said the foreman.

'*She* won't be sorry, either.'

'It'll be a shock, Michael,' said the foreman gently. 'Don't forget that.'

'He was murdered.' Doyle's tone carried no surprise.

'Good Lord!'

'I should have murdered him years ago. It would have saved the old lady a lot of grief.' Michael Doyle placed the power-saw carefully on the grass. He added: 'I'll be back to drop the elm before we finish for the day.'

'Take . . .' The foreman swallowed. 'Take your time, Michael. It'll wait.'

9

'Not all that difficult.'

That's how the Head of CID had described a murder inquiry – as being 'not all that difficult', for God's sake!

Lyle sat in his office and gradually realised the basic truth of what the DCS had said. Indeed, it was *not* going to be 'all that difficult'. It was going to be ridiculously easy – up to a point. An arrest on suspicion could take place now. This very minute. The lifting of a telephone receiver would take the murderer out of circulation. But only temporarily.

An arrest, but no charge. And, if anybody was crazy enough to press for a charge, not a cat in hell's chance of a conviction without evidence.

It was, Lyle decided, the most cock-eyed murder inquiry he'd ever tangled with. A killing where the killer was known but where proof was nonexistent was a most peculiar ballgame. It meant being both devious and certain. It meant probing for weaknesses until some sort of breaking-point was reached.

'Not all that difficult.'

Not if *you* didn't have to do it. Not if *you* didn't have to divert the attention of the quarry while, at the same time, building and baiting some near-impossible trap.

Lyle lit a cigarette and allowed the sour thoughts freedom of his mind.

Come the end – come the headlines – and the general public would swallow everything they were fed. Doyle would get the sympathetic treatment, because Doyle had been murdered. That the world in general, and Rogate-on-Sands in particular, was a better place *without* Doyle wouldn't even be hinted at. Some red-hot news editor would sort through photographs and come up with one which made the murderer look like an escapee from Bedlam.

That, for sure. That's what *always* happened.

Doyle, on the other hand . . .

A poor misunderstood teenager. An unfortunate whose high jinks had made him an enemy of evil-minded killjoys.

The cops couldn't win. Lyle couldn't win. The whole bloody set-up stank of a subtle corruption in which lies and half-truths were manipulated for the sake of circulation. *Not* to send the killer to prison meant being accused of inefficiency. Doing what, eventually, *had* to be done elevated a young tearaway to the status of near-martyr.

The telephone on his desk broke Lyle's dark musings.

The media he'd been mentally cursing were at the public counter. Reporters from surrounding districts. The local television and radio interviewers.

'They want to know, sir.' The constable at the public counter sounded a little desperate. 'They're waiting for some sort of official statement.'

'Tell them to contact Force Headquarters,' growled Lyle. 'Tell them to consult our own Lords of Creation. Meanwhile contact Detective Inspector Faber and ask him to get to my office as soon as possible.'

10

Police Constable 417 Gul had visions of glory. He had done far more than 'slip a jacket on, instead of the tunic'. He had also changed the tie from standard black issue to a rather fetching light blue, with dark stripes.

'It should go well with the police shirt.'

Nor had he been satisfied with his everyday chunky sweater and zip-up. To his wife's surprise he'd plumped for a rather nifty, recently dry-cleaned Norfolk jacket and a belted mac of a distinct 'Humphrey Bogart' cut.

He looked more like a Hollywood private eye than an English provincial pavement-basher.

'D'you think I need a hat?' He made it a very serious question.

'Gully, old luv.' The young lady to whom he'd asked the question allowed laughter to lilt her voice. 'All you're going to do is knock on a few doors and ask a few questions. You're not flogging double-glazing.'

'You want me to get on, don't you?' The question carried a hint of outraged surprise.

'Of course I want you to get on. And you *will*. . . .'

'It's a *murder* inquiry.'

'I know. Jimmy Doyle. And good—'

'And *I* found the body.'

'Strictly speaking – as you've told me half a dozen times – you had the body pointed out to you.'

'I was the first officer at the scene – and that's very important.'

'If you say so.'

'And now the super's told me to change into plain clothes.'

'Fine.'

'So – y'know – I want to *look* the part.'

'What "part"?'

'It's my case,' explained Gul.

'Eh?'

'I don't want to trail along looking like a poor relation.'

'Gully, my pet.' She was a few months younger than her husband yet, wife-like, her tone was that of a mother giving guidance to a well-loved child. 'Don't expect too much, luv. Don't over-react. These people – these sergeants, inspectors, chief inspectors – they're not going to let *you* take over.'

'Oh, I don't want to *take over*. It's just that . . .'

'Stay in the background, luv. Don't let them . . .'

She stopped and closed her mouth. She'd been going to say 'laugh at you', but that would have been wrong. Even cruel.

'Don't let them what?' Gul looked puzzled.

'Put on you,' she said lamely. 'Don't let them put on you.'

Her choice of phrase gave hint of her origins, as did the slight flatness of her dialect. Blackburn born. Lancashire, from top to toe. She'd 'wed a black man' in the idiom of the neighbourhood in which she'd lived. It had given her the status of someone not far removed from a whore, and with the gradual realisation had come mystification and shock.

Jan Gul was a chap she'd met while holidaying in Blackpool. One Wakes Week. He'd been a cadet, up the coast in Rogate-on-Sands. They'd liked each other. They'd written to each other. They'd visited each other, then they'd fallen in love.

What else, but to marry?

Neither had been conscious of the other's colour. The only teasing banter they'd indulged in had been of the

31

Yorkshire–Lancashire kind. The two Rose Counties. Which was the best.

The more-than-hinted-at prejudice of friends and neighbours had outraged the then Pam Sugden, and it had taken the solid wisdom of her widowed father to hold her world steady.

'Pam, lass, his colour's nowt to do with it. If he's a good man – if he's good to *you* – that's all that matters. Happen the others are a bit jealous. Happen they wish *they* had a man as good as Gully.'

It had always been 'Gully'. Never 'Jan'. It was what his mates called him, and that had been good enough for her.

And yet . . .

Marriage, as always, had exposed weaknesses, but the weaknesses had nothing to do with skin pigmentation. What had once seemed pride in appearance was now a mildly irritating over-attention to dress. Punctiliousness in doing everything correctly was now an annoying obsession to get everything book-perfect.

'I might need my truncheon,' Gul was saying.

'What?'

'My truncheon. I might need it, if I have to arrest a murderer.'

'It's possible,' sighed his wife.

'A pity, really. Otherwise I'd have changed trousers. Uniform trousers don't go with this jacket.'

'For God's sake, Gully.'

'I need the truncheon-pocket.' Gul misunderstood his wife's remark. 'I might *need* the truncheon.'

'You might.'

'But there's nowhere to put it if I don't wear uniform trousers.'

'You look all right.' She used a flat emotionless tone. 'You look fine. You don't need a hat. You'll do a good job . . . I'm sure you will.'

32

'Eh? Oh . . . of course.' He seemed surprised that the remark had been called for.

11

'You all right, Mammy?' Michael Doyle dwarfed his mother, but seemed shy and tongue-tied. 'Is there anything *I* can do?'

'And many's the long moon since you asked *that* question, Michael Doyle.' The implied accusation was only half-hearted.

'Mammy . . . you know why.'

'And now he's dead, you want to wheedle your way back in here. Is that it?'

The giant shook his head and looked infinitely sad.

'You'll not be telling me you're here to mourn him, are you?'

'That would be a lie, Mammy.'

' "Mammy! Mammy!"' she mocked gently.

'And what else should I call you? What else have I *ever* called you?'

'You're a softie, Michael Doyle, so you are.'

'I'm not like *he* was,' he agreed.

'No.' A gentle smile touched her lips, and she shook her head slowly. 'You're a good son, Michael. And it's me that doesn't appreciate it.'

'Without him here I could have looked after you.'

'Ay . . . and you would, too. I don't doubt that.'

He cleared his throat, then in a low voice said: 'I'm glad he's dead, Mammy. He should have been put under the sod years ago. It's where he belongs.'

'You shouldn't say such things about your own brother,

33

Michael Doyle. He was a wild one – like his father – that's all.'

'And me?' he asked gently.

'I'll make you some tea.' She changed the subject abruptly. 'We'll sit and talk a while.'

'Ay. That would be nice.'

They talked for more than an hour. They exchanged memories and relived moments of years ago. Some of his timidity left him and, for her part, she became less restrained. Occasionally, they even laughed.

As he stood up to leave he felt in his hip pocket. He placed a slim bundle of ten- and five-pound notes on the mantelpiece.

'Seventy-five pounds,' he murmured. 'It's all I could lay my hands on. . . .'

'Look, son, I don't need . . .'

'Telephone Uncle Patrick. Arrange something. I'll take care of things at this end.'

'Look . . .'

'He's dead, Mammy. Don't waste good Irish tears.'

12

Superintendent Robert Crosby disliked murder inquiries.

He wasn't too damn keen on murder, come to that, but if people jockeyed themselves into a position where they were done to death that was *their* fault. It was the resultant *inquiries* that upset Crosby. They knocked the rota system to hell. If they were like the one last year they brought snide remarks from the local media clowns. And if – again like the one last year – the fornicating thing stayed 'undetected' the Chief Constable had a nasty

34

habit of winging very pointed missives in the direction of Rogate-on-Sands.

He wasn't prepared to go through *that* little lot again.

'Sort this one out, Lyle.' Crosby's tone carried anger neatly framed by a desperate plea.

'I've already sent for Detective Inspector Faber.'

'The buck stops with you, Lyle, not Faber.'

'Of course.'

'I want it detecting.'

'Superintendent.' Smile-lines webbed the corner of Lyle's eyes. 'For you . . . anything.'

Crosby didn't like Lyle's eyes. They were too penetrating by half. Babies were born with forget-me-not blue eyes but, normally, age brought a shade-change. It hadn't with Lyle. The same blue was still there, but more cold and more piercing.

Dammit, they were *intimidating*.

'Lyle,' insisted Crosby, 'I'm serious.'

'So am I.'

'It's not that *I* mind. . . .'

'*I* mind.'

'It's just that the old man gets very prickly if we don't perform miracles.'

'Not miracles.' Lyle's voice was deceptively gentle. 'We do the job. We do our best. We are *not* miracle-workers.'

Crosby grunted and stared his worry past the car window and through the convenient gap in Rock Walk. Past the prom and out to sea to where the body of Doyle had been washed ashore.

'The bloody man,' he complained. 'Trouble alive. Even *more* trouble now he's dead.'

'Some people might be quite jubilant.'

'Well, *I'm* not.'

Crosby was there under slight protest. He worked on the theory that the less he 'knew' the less fertiliser could be shunted in his direction. This little lot was murder. It

35

was CID territory, therefore it was Lyle's pigeon.

Lyle had been adamant.

'You should visit the scene, Superintendent. Show your face. At least *pretend* some degree of interest.'

'Of course I'm interested.'

'Of *course* you are,' Lyle had mocked.

'This is my division.'

'Quite.'

And, as always, Lyle had had his way. It was another of Lyle's tricks. To be able to move men, of whatever rank, like a grand master moving chess-pieces. So many bloody pawns! It was damned annoying but, so far, nobody seemed to have come up with a way of blocking him. 'Lyle's Way.' That's what they called it in the canteens and bars of the force. Not the official way. Not the police way. Not the textbook way. Just . . . 'Lyle's Way.'

Crosby felt a flush of anger at this angular knuckle-boned detective chief inspector who seemed to have answers where lesser men had to make do with questions.

He snapped: 'I don't have to remind you, Lyle. You weren't good enough last year.'

'Mary Sutcliffe?'

'That's one case you *couldn't* bottom.'

'Couldn't *prove*,' murmured Lyle smoothly. 'We know who murdered her. To *that* extent we succeeded.'

'You mean . . .' Crosby's mouth hung slack for a moment. Lyle had done it again! He gasped: 'You mean to sit there and tell me you can put a name to the bastard who— ?'

'Of course.' Lyle corrected himself. '*Some* of us. For obvious reasons the knowledge wasn't for public consumption.'

'I'm not "public", Lyle.' Crosby's face darkened. His eyes glared. 'Damnation, I'm the blasted divisional officer. If anybody should have been told—'

'What good would it have done?'

'Good. *Good!* It isn't a matter of—'

36

'Superintendent, you didn't see *that* corpse, either.' Lyle cut into Crosby's outrage with a tone on a par with iced water being thrown on smouldering ashes. 'As I recall, you visited the incident centre only once. To insist that some of the uniformed men be returned to the beat. To give motorists parked on double yellow lines – and I quote – "a short sharp lesson".'

'Good God, man. Had I known—'

'You didn't *want* to know, Superintendent. You kept the whole inquiry at arm's length. The file was completed, as far as possible, then submitted. *You* didn't even glance at it.' Lyle's tone became even smoother. Even more menacing. 'If you doubt what I'm saying – if you insist you were even half-interested in who murdered Mary Sutcliffe – we'll drive to Force Headquarters. Now. This minute. We'll take the Sutcliffe file from wherever it is and, if you've as much as *initialled* it to show it crossed your desk. . . .'

Lyle left the sentence unfinished, but the moment or two of silence was enough.

'I'm a divisional officer,' croaked Crosby.

'That's what you're paid for being,' agreed Lyle.

'I've a lot on my plate.'

'Haven't we all?'

'There's always *something*.'

'Double yellow lines, for example,' mocked Lyle.

'One day,' breathed Crosby. 'One day, Lyle, you'll come unstuck.'

'It's not impossible.'

'You'll be out there, on a limb.'

'And you, Superintendent Crosby, will be there with a woodman's saw, working harder than you've ever worked in your life.'

'Bet on it, Lyle,' rasped Crosby. '*Bet* on it.'

13

Percy 'Boy' Hammond couldn't stop shaking.

Ever since the news, then the verification, that Jimmy Doyle's strangled body had been washed up on the beach Hammond had been unable to control the trembling. He'd left the stainless-steel-topped table where he worked alongside more skilled employees. He'd wandered through various store-rooms, like a man lost in a maze. The sweet sugary smell of the rock factory had made him want to puke and, for a few minutes, he'd stepped out into the yard at the back to gulp fresh air.

Now he was in the bog, with the door locked and the seat-cover down. He stared at the crudely drawn genitalia on the whitewashed walls and the dirty rhymes and remarks scrawled beneath. He stared beyond the grubby walls and saw again – for the thousandth time – an elderly woman mugged to death. The blood from the head wound and from the face. The murder he had once been party to.

He sat and trembled as the year-old panic once more engulfed him.

He'd thought he'd finished with it. He'd thought he could gradually push it farther and farther back into his memory. Never quite forget it, but not *remember* it as often as he once had.

And now this.

Doyle's murdered body washed up on the beach and, again, the bloody coppers leaning for a cough. This time the sods would *really* lean. This time they'd *never* be satisfied.

Trickles of sweat ran down the sides of his face and

converged into a drop at his chin. The drop fell as he ran his fingers through his damp hair.

'You bastard,' he breathed. 'You stupid, *stupid* bastard. Why did you have to be washed ashore?'

14

In Lyle's office Detective Inspector Frank Faber listened to what Lyle believed to be the truth. He listened in silence.

Then he said: 'Hearsay *of* hearsay.'

'We need proof,' agreed Lyle.

'As sure as hell we need *something*.'

'We need evidence.'

'No. What we really need, Chief Inspector, is a bloody miracle.'

Lyle said: 'All we have so far is motive.'

'*Possible* motive.'

'Everything,' argued Lyle, 'points to Doyle and his pal Hammond murdering Mary Sutcliffe – right?'

Faber nodded.

'We hadn't enough proof on that one, either – remember?'

'Are we talking about vigilante stuff?'

'No.'

'Because if we are . . .'

'We are *not*,' said Lyle firmly. 'Michael Winner might approve of the "Death Wish" theme, but in Rogate-on-Sands it's a non-starter.'

'Therefore?' Faber raised quizzical eyebrows.

'I'm bringing Frome in from Pullbury, to work with Sergeant Jackson. They're buddies – them *and* their wives

– and, between them, they might pull something off.'
'And my job?'
'Freelance. Street-level co-ordinator.'
'Flash words . . . meaning "watcher".'
'With me out there everybody would be too careful.
With you – apparently *not* knowing the details – somebody
might make a mistake.'
'Just a dumb detective inspector, mooching about with
his eyes closed.'
'It's the name of this game, Frank. It has to be.'

15

It was moving up to one o'clock, and Bob Jackson had
nipped home for a quick meal. He knew it was going to
be an unhappy meal, because so many of his meals – so
much of his *life* – had been unhappy for months.

Muriel seemed unable to accept the trigger-horror of
it all. She'd never recovered or, it seemed, even *tried*
to recover from that first shock. And now things were
worse.

Before there had been a perpetual numbness in her
behaviour. Now a strange petrified terror had pushed her
even deeper into this pit of her own making.

She was a good wife. Despite everything, she was *still*
a good wife. Despite the drugs, despite her inability to
communicate, despite the apparent impossibility of her
ever being happy again, she remained a good wife.

A year ago he'd have described her as 'the best wife in
the world', and would have meant it.

He toyed with the smoked haddock and poached egg

she'd provided for a meal. He sat alone in the dining-alcove of the neat semi they'd once been so proud of. He heard her moving in the adjoining kitchen, but guessed she was finding work in order to avoid joining him.

Very softly, but in a tight voice, he called: 'It's what you wanted, Muriel.'

She didn't answer.

He sipped tea, then pushed the still half-filled plate away.

He called: 'Muriel. It's what you've been *praying* for, for almost a year.'

She appeared at the open door of the kitchen. Her face was pale and strained, with dark half-moons under her eyes. Her voice was little more than a whisper, and she rested one hand against the jamb as if to steady herself.

'It's *not* what I wanted, Bob.'

'Oh, yes.' He nodded wearily.

'Not the *way* I wanted it.'

'It's what you *wanted*,' he insisted.

'I wanted him dead. I wanted both of them dead. I *wished* them both to die. I even *prayed* for them to die, but . . .'

'Part of your prayer has been answered.' He raised his head and stared at her, his eyes filled with hurt. 'You're *still* not satisfied.'

'Bob!'

For a moment, they gazed at each other. Two people still very much in love, but unable to reach each other. Each desperate to make the other understand. Each unable to do so.

Jackson lowered his eyes and allowed his out-of-focus gaze to stare into the middle distance. There was a strange emotion in his words. A negative emotion, with smouldering heat but no fire. He seemed to be mouthing the words to himself.

41

'They killed her, Muriel. They murdered your mother and broke *your* heart. You hated them both – Doyle and Hammond – oh, how you hated them! Both of them. The number of times you've *wished* them dead. It's what should have happened to them. Both of them. The hanging-shed – it shouldn't have been abolished. And now Doyle's got his deserts. He's been murdered. And Hammond's scared out of his wits – he must be.'

'Not this,' she whispered. 'Not *this*.'

'What else?' His tone remained the same. His eyes remained out of focus. 'Two cretinous bastards hammer an elderly woman to death for the sake of a few spare quid. *God Almighty!* And they got away with it. They made you like you are. Like you've been since it happened. They've dragged you through hell. Me, too. And they walked the streets, free men. For lack of evidence.' He took a deep breath and expelled the air in one long shuddering sigh. 'No way, Muriel. No *way*. This one, too, is going to stay "undetected". I'll see to that . . . personally.'

She breathed: 'They'll catch you, Bob. They'll find out. They'll send you to prison . . . then I'll have *nobody*.'

'Muriel.' Very slowly, he raised his eyes and looked at her face. His voice was soft and soothing. Comforting and certain. 'Muriel . . . try to understand. Two yobs – two thick-skulled ignorant louts – killed your mother. *And we couldn't prove it.* We hadn't enough evidence to take them to court. Because of so-called "subjectivity", I wasn't allowed to be on that case. But I'm on *this* one. In the middle of it all. This one, too, stays "undetected". I swear. Every lead blocked. Every mistake rectified before it can mean anything. I'm in there – part of the inquiry – I'll know *exactly* what's going on. For heaven's sake, Muriel, my pet . . . there's nothing to worry about.'

16

Once upon a time they were called 'murder rooms'. Then, because it was less intimidating, they were called 'incident rooms'. Now they glory in the even more flash name of 'incident centres'. Their purpose remains the same – permanent or mobile: they are where the wheat and the chaff, the garbage and the gold, are sorted and assessed. They are still called 'murder rooms' by the more ancient men of law-enforcement. Equally, they are often called 'incident rooms'.

Who the hell cares? The chaos remains as old-fashioned as ever.

Number One Incident Centre was losing its pristine glitter. The typewriters, lugged in from Headquarters Store and from section stations and sub-divisional offices, weren't new. They weren't even electric. The handful of statements and reports already completed were scattered about surfaces waiting to be numbered, tagged, cross-referenced, then filed. For the moment, only a few. Eventually they could number hundreds or even thousands.

A sergeant clerk, two constable clerks and a cadet busied themselves checking that the required forms, tags and scribbling-pads were both plentiful and available.

A British Telecom engineer was fixing extra handsets to points already available along the skirting-boards.

In short the glossy-surfaced tranquillity upon which the architect had recently smiled was having a necessary face-lift. Architects are not coppers, and everything had *not* been 'taken care of'.

43

Small, but important, things were missing.

The sergeant clerk glanced up at the strip-lighting and gave instructions to the cadet.

'A couple of spare neon tubes, old son. And a couple of those starter gadgets that get the light going. Buzz stores. Tell 'em we want them this afternoon. Two o'clock in the morning, and if the lighting goes on the blink somebody's arse is going to be in a sling.'

'And a carton of new typewriter ribbons,' called one of the constable clerks. '*And* a few packs of carbon paper.'

'This bloody place,' grumbled the sergeant clerk. 'It's as much use as a Rolls-Royce with an empty tank.'

The cadet didn't mind playing general dogsbody. He was a cheerful lad, and this *was* a murder inquiry. Real 'Hill Street Blues' stuff. We-ell – maybe not quite as hectic as his favourite television programme, but something he'd be able to tell his mum and dad about when next he visited his home in Huddersfield.

The sergeant clerk, on the other hand, had been at a couple of previous 'murder room' pantomimes. He knew how things developed. Little things – like *your* goolies being caught in somebody else's rat-trap.

Given time, tempers became very razor-edged. A paper-clip that wasn't immediately available could trigger of something approaching the Third World War. A snapped pencil-point, a ballpoint running dry – these things, not whizz-bang filing systems, made the difference between tranquillity and high drama.

He opened one of the windows. The lingering whiff of fresh paint was something else likely to be blown up out of all proportion when the promising leads dead-ended, when the arches ached and when mouths had the taste of a Turkish wrestler's jock-strap.

The very shine of Number One Incident Centre was enough to sour men who'd worked themselves to exhaustion-point without moving an inch.

'You're on first spell.' He spoke to one of the constable clerks. 'Pass the word. Watch out for Crosby.'

'Crosby?' The constable looked surprised.

'Our dearly beloved superintendent. I've left word with the Charge Office. They'll give us a bell if he points his nose in this direction.'

'Is it likely?'

'Everybody,' said the sergeant clerk heavily. 'Every medal-chaser this side of the moon.'

'Crosby? Chasing medals?'

'Believe me. Crosby will be around, scooping up any gash gongs going. That, or making damn sure nobody else does.'

17

Lyle skipped lunch. Instead, he drove out to Pullbury.

Pullbury was within the Rogate-on-Sands Division. It was a one-sergeant-six-constable section, set back from the coast and embracing a scattering of villages and hamlets sprinkled across rolling farmland.

The uniformed sergeant responsible for the running of Pullbury Section was Jim Frome.

Frome and Lyle strolled in the garden at the rear of the Sergeant's house. The garden was large enough to merit the description of 'allotment', but that was OK. Frome was a keen gardener.

'It doesn't often happen, does it, Sergeant?' said Lyle mildly.

'What's that, sir?'

'To know who the murderer is before we have a corpse?'

Frome looked uncomfortable.

The yard-wide path of pine needles led past a metal-framed greenhouse, and Frome pushed open the sliding door then stood back to allow Lyle to enter. The interior of the greenhouse smelt of peat, and the ring-cultured tomato plants were already in position on the gravel-surfaced bench.

Frome muttered: 'I could have got hold of the wrong end of things, sir.'

'Possible,' agreed Lyle.

'I don't pretend to be particularly bright.' Frome touched the loose gravel with the tips of his fingers. 'I make mistakes.'

'We all make mistakes, Sergeant.'

'What I mean is . . .'

'On the other hand, we don't all get that sort of a tip-off.'

'No, sir,' sighed Frome.

Lyle bent to sniff the faint pungency of a tiny tomato plant. As he straightened he said: 'A very unhappy state of affairs, Sergeant.'

'Sir . . .' Frome closed his mouth.

'Yes?'

'Can I – can I be kept out of things?'

'No.'

'I mean, if it's at all possible. . . .'

'It's not at all possible, Sergeant'.

'No, sir,' breathed Frome.

'It was right of you to pass the information on to me.'

'Everything seems "right", sir. . . if you see what I mean.'

'Of course. But, also, very *wrong*.'

'Yes, sir.' Frome's teeth were tightly clenched.

In a gentle tone Lyle asked: 'The truth, Sergeant . . . are you frightened?'

'Yes, sir. Very.'

'So am I, Sergeant. So am I.'

'Doyle was an evil bastard, sir.' Passion touched Frome's tone. 'Even out here, we all knew *that*.'

'That he was.'

'Killing Bob Jackson's mother-in-law. It drove Muriel out of her mind.'

'Sergeant Jackson has had a very rough time,' agreed Lyle.

'I've seen it at close quarters, sir.' Some of the passion was replaced by sadness. 'Muriel – Mrs Jackson – should have had specialised treatment.'

'But she didn't?'

'She refused.'

'It happens, Sergeant. Very often.'

For a few moments Lyle stared through the glass of the greenhouse, towards where the first rise of the Pennines was blurred in the haze of distance. His face was quite expressionless. It showed neither friendship nor enmity; neither weakness nor strength; neither compassion nor disgust. When he spoke, he continued to stare at the distant skyline and his voice matched his expression.

'We both hated Doyle for what he'd done to Mrs Sutcliffe. We both know what happened – that Hammond was *there*, but wasn't much more than Doyle's lackey – and we both know that Doyle couldn't be touched. The evidence wasn't available. Agreed?'

'Yes, sir.'

'But that doesn't matter a damn. What Doyle *was* – what Doyle *did* – isn't important. Doyle's been murdered. Only *that* matters.'

Frome remained silent, and waited.

'Therefore, we play a game, Sergeant Frome.' Lyle brought his gaze from the distant hills and stared at the uniformed sergeant. 'You and I – with our special knowledge – play a game.'

'I'll do whatever you say, sir.'

'That you will.' A quick tight smile touched Lyle's lips.

'Your future depends on it. Your *future* – and not necessarily only in the police service.'

'Yes, sir.' The two words carried complete capitulation.

'This one is going to be detected,' said Lyle. 'We are not having two duds on the trot.' He paused, then continued: 'There will be evidence . . . somewhere. Clues. Enough clues – enough evidence – to make it stick. Detective Sergeant Jackson is part of the inquiry team . . . naturally. You, Sergeant Frome, will work alongside him. Any attempt at destroying evidence, covering up clues – I want to know. That's your job. To let me know if Jackson tries to spike a successful conclusion.'

Frome's fingers closed on a handful of gravel. He allowed it to trickle back into place before he spoke.

'Have I a choice, sir?' he whispered.

'None.' Then, with some degree of sympathy: 'He's your friend. What Doyle did to his wife's mother – what Doyle did to Jackson's wife – does not make for pleasant contemplation. But you, too, have a wife . . . right?'

'Yes, sir.'

'If,' said Lyle, 'the temptation to ally yourself with Sergeant Jackson becomes too strong – think of *her*.'

Frome croaked: 'Yes, sir.'

18

Kate Doyle returned home having visited a telephone kiosk.

She smoked a cigarette and pondered upon life without the burden of her younger son. Life without the constant worry that, one day, he'd overstep the mark and do something even *she* couldn't forgive.

And yet . . .

Damn the child, he *had* done. Dozens of times. Scores of times. He'd had the devil of his father in him since he'd been born, and he'd never made any effort to change his ways. He'd been a bully, a liar and a coward. His father had broken her heart, and her younger son had heeled the broken heart into pulp.

Last year poor old Mrs Sutcliffe had been mugged to death. A nice soul, killed in a shameful way. A wicked thing, and the police had taken Jimmy in for questioning. They'd kept him inside for twelve long hours. Him and that silly Hammond youth. Then he'd come home, cocky and bad-tempered.

And, God forgive her, she'd *known*. He'd denied it, with all the foul and filthy language he could lay his tongue to, but she'd known. She was his mother. He could lie to the police and make them believe his lies, but he couldn't lie to his own mother and make *her* believe.

She'd learned to watch for little things. The movement of his eyes when he talked. The way he cracked the knuckles of his right hand. The way he sneered down any suggestion that he wasn't telling the truth.

She'd *known*!

Dear God, she'd given birth to a monster.

And now he was dead. In the old days they'd have hanged him, and now he'd *been* hanged. A rope around his neck, and no less than he'd deserved.

She was surprised to find that her cigarette had gone out. She stared at it for a moment. It was damp and soggy. The paper was almost transparent. She raised her free hand and touched her cheek.

She became aware of the tears. Streams of tears which wet both her cheeks.

'Damn you, Jimmy Doyle,' she sobbed. 'Damn you to hell, with your no-good father. And it's your poor old mother who's wishing it. You were bad, Jimmy. Holy

Mother of God, you were *bad*. I'll make no more excuses for you. That I won't. You got what you deserved . . . and I'm *glad*.'

19

Police Constable 417 Gul figured he'd drawn the short straw, and was very annoyed.

At first he'd made token protest.

He'd said: 'Sergeant, this is *my* case.'

'Eh?' Bob Jackson had stared non-understanding.

'I found the body,' Gul had explained.

'So? Somebody had to find the bloody thing.'

'I was the first officer at the scene.'

'Somebody had to be *that*, too.'

'Sergeant, that makes it *my* case.'

Jackson had stared his disbelief for a moment, then growled: 'Gul, don't be a bigger prat than God made you.'

'Look, you've no right to—'

'On your way, Gul.' Jackson's stare had hardened into a glare. 'You're here to obey orders. This is a team effort, lad . . . and *you* are a very unimportant member of that team.'

And that had been that, and Gul could think of no way to buck a very unfair system. Which was why he was pushing his way through a continuingly stiff breeze, moving from one hotel lobby to the next. He'd been lumbered with a typical Forth Bridge job. Covering every establishment with a window which overlooked the sea.

He punched the bell on the 'Enquiries' counter and waited.

A shrimp of a man whose hairpiece was slightly askew and who wore crumpled grey slacks and a black waistcoat over a white shirt arrived from some mysterious region beyond the lobby.

'We're not an all-year-round establishment.' He was talking before he reached the counter. He was obviously in an ill-temper. 'Dammit, there's a "No Vacancies" sign as big as a hoarding on the front door. Anyway, the door shouldn't have been unlocked. It must have been—'

'Police.' Gul interrupted the flow, and at the same time slapped his warrant-card on the counter with some authority.

'Oh!'

'I'd like to see—'

'I've already told you. There's nobody *staying* here. We'll have the fire-doors installed before we open for the season. I don't know what the hell . . .' The man had been examining the warrant-card. Now he stopped talking, raised his head, seemed to notice Gul's face for the first time, and muttered: 'Good God!'

'What's that?'

'A coloured rozzer.'

'A *what*?' Gul's jaw muscles tightened.

'Y'know . . .' A mildly gormless smile twitched the man's lips. 'Not many about, are there? I didn't know *we* had one.'

'Now you *do* know,' snapped Gul.

'Anyway – the fire-doors. . . .' The man's tone was airily dismissive. 'I've already arranged for—'

'*Not* the fire-doors.' Gul's tone was not at all friendly. 'The Fire Service handle fire-doors.'

'Oh!'

'Murder.'

'I – I . . .'

'A body washed up on the beach, earlier today. A murder victim.'

'You're having me *on*.'

'I'm not having you on.' Gul retrieved the warrant-card and opened his notebook. 'What's your name, mister?'

The man's eyes widened. He raised a hand, touched the hairpiece and pushed it even more askew.

'Your name?' repeated Gul.

'It's – er – LeFage.'

'LeFage.' As he wrote the name, Gul murmured: 'Such a very English name. And the first name?'

'Leo. Max Leo.'

'Max . . . Leo . . . LeFage.' Gul rolled the unusual names around, as if flavouring their strangeness. He was a Yorkshireman. He took just so much slop from *anybody*. He added: 'And *you* think *I'm* unusual.'

'Look, you've no right to—'

'What's the name of this boarding-house?'

'Boarding-house! This is a *hotel*. This isn't a—'

'What's it's name?'

'The Brookside.'

Gul recorded the name. He took his time, then he asked: 'How many rooms facing the sea?'

'Am I allowed to know what all this infernal nonsense is about?'

'Murder.' Gul was enjoying showing his teeth. 'The victim was washed up, earlier today. . . .'

'You've already said that.'

'My job is to check all rooms with a window which overlooks the sea.'

'I've already told you, Constable What-the-hell-your-name-is. . . .'

'Gul.'

'Constable Gul. I've already told you, this hotel is *not* open out of season.'

'Rooms,' said Gul flatly. 'Windows. Not guests. Those are my orders. And, Mr Max Leo LeFage, *that* is exactly what I'm going to do.' Gul hesitated a moment, then took

52

the plunge and added: 'With, or without, a warrant.'

Gul wasn't a copper given to chancing his arm, but this LeFage character was crawling right up his nostrils. Nor was this case on a par with nicking milk-bottles. It was *his* case, and it was *murder*.

LeFage, on the other hand, was a creep whose whole life was built on shifting sand. He had certain ambitions within the orbit of authoritarianism but, unfortunately, his appearance got in the way. Almost always he ended up with egg dripping from his chin.

About thirty minutes later Gul had been shown into every bedroom on the four floors which made up the guest-quarters of the Brookside. Poky rooms. Each with its washbasin. Each with its cheap beds and its even cheaper wardrobe.

'What's beyond there?' Gul nodded towards a door marked 'Private'.

'That's where *I* live.'

'Another storey?'

'A dormer room, actually. None of the guests—'

'The window looks out to sea.' Gul turned his head to check, then added: 'Yes . . . it must look out to sea.'

'For Christ's sake!'

'Every window looking out to sea,' said Gul flatly.

'There's only my bed and a few bits and pieces,' protested LeFage.

The protest was too immediate. Too urgent. It suggested something Le Fage wasn't keen on Gul seeing.

Gul said: 'It's the window I'm interested in. *Every* window . . . that's what my orders are. I'll make a quick check.'

Reluctantly LeFage opened the door and led the way up the final flight of stairs.

It was a small room and it reflected the interests of its owner. Four hard-porn posters occupied pride of place on the walls. A cheap bookcase was stuffed with paperbacks, most of which were English and American examples of fornicatory story-telling. A pile of girlie magazines were on the carpet alongside the unmade double bed.

'Married?' asked Gul idly.

'If it's any business of yours—'

'It isn't.'

' —we're separated.'

'That follows.'

'Look!' LeFage tried outraged indignation for size. 'I don't have to listen to some smartarse copper . . .'

'Watch it, LeFage,' warned Gul.

'What I do in the privacy of my own home is *my* affair.'

'Is it?'

'There's nothing illegal about—'

'Don't be too sure about those posters.'

'That's *art*. Those things are damned expensive.'

'Aye. So are good-class dirty postcards.'

Gul strolled to the window. A top-quality telescope stood on its tripod, with its large lens almost touching the glass.

'Ships?' asked Gul mockingly.

'Eh?'

'Or people undressing on the beach?'

'Do what you're here to do,' snarled LeFage. 'After that, mind your own bloody business.'

'You', said Gul coldly, 'are a dirty-minded little runt. One question, though.' He touched the telescope. 'Were you looking through this thing this morning?'

'No.'

'Not trying to catch an eyeful of what you shouldn't be looking at?'

'No.' There was sulky defeat in the repeated denial. All pretence of indignation had gone. LeFage wanted Gul out of his life. He muttered: 'I didn't see a thing. I didn't even look. Now, get off my premises and leave me alone.'

54

20

Some women are natural police wives. They can appreciate that, at times, their old man is harried from pillar to post and that, when he staggers home, the last thing he needs is a did-you-have-a-good-day-at-the-office-darling routine. They are conscious of the lunatics, the kinks, the creeps and the scum which requires his presence on the street. They know that daily – almost hourly – he is in contact with idiots and morons. They appreciate that, having slammed the front door, all he yearns for is elbow-room in which to take a few deep breaths in the hope that oxygen input might encourage some degree of normality.

Such wives are worth their weight in diamonds to a working copper. They know when to talk and know what to say. More important, they know when *not* to talk. They can sense when the long-suffering boy has heard far too much talk and now yearns for large lumps of soft soothing silence.

They can spot the mood instantly, and have the wisdom to act accordingly.

Joyce Frome was not one of them.

This is not to say that Mrs Frome *disliked* being the wife of Police Sergeant Frome. She rather liked it. It carried status in the Pullbury Women's Institute.

Nor, as a wife, had she too many faults. She could cook reasonably well. She kept a clean and moderately tidy home. She'd presented her husband with three fine kids, all of whom had now flown the cote to live their own lives. As a wife, she was a success – but not as a *police* wife.

This was something Sergeant Frome was beginning to realise.

When Jim Frome had met her she'd been bouncy. Cuddly. A happy bundle of innocent kiss-me-quick fun.

Now she was overweight. Well overweight.

Not that her size meant much. Her hubby still loved her, and there was more of her to love. She still laughed readily and without vulgarity. Despite her size she retained that strange daintiness sometimes found in overweight people.

She knew her age and dressed her age, without being frumpy. She drank a little, but never got drunk. She smoked no more than five cigarettes a day. Not once had she even *thought* of two-timing her husband.

All this . . . but she talked too much. *Far* too much, for a copper's wife.

She was, for example, talking to a neighbour she'd met on her way back from Pullbury post office.

'. . . and Jim's been pulled in to help with the inquiry.'

'Has he?'

'I don't know when I'll see him next. These things go on and on.'

'Yes . . . I suppose they do.'

'Everybody has to be seen, over and over again. Statements and things.'

'But very interesting . . . surely?'

'Well, you see, it's three weeks since it happened.'

'Is it? I thought it happened today. That—'

'No, I mean it's three weeks since Doyle went missing.'

'Oh, I didn't know that.'

'They didn't know he'd been *murdered* until today.'

'Oh!'

'A terrible man.'

'Who?'

'Doyle. Jimmy Doyle. A really *terrible* person. The things I could tell you.'

'I didn't know. I didn't know him at all.'

'Oh, an absolute *animal*. I mean – y'know – Mrs Sutcliffe.'

56

'Mrs Sutcliffe?'

'Mary Sutcliffe. The lady who was murdered about a year ago.'

'Oh . . . *her*.'

'I knew her well. I've known her daughter for years.'

'Really?'

'I mean, it's an open secret that Jimmy Doyle murdered *her*.'

'Jimmy Doyle! The man they've found . . . ?'

'Oh, an open secret. But the police couldn't *prove* anything.'

'Good heavens!'

'I mean, an animal that does *that* doesn't deserve any sympathy, does he?'

'Not if what you say is right.'

'Oh, it's right all right.'

'Well, in that case . . .'

'That's why the police will put up a *show*.'

'How d'you mean?'

'Well, they aren't really bothered, are they? Why *should* they be?'

'Ah, yes. But if—'

'I mean, they'll make something of a fuss, of course.'

'A fuss?'

'A show. Putting on a show.'

'Oh!'

'It's what they're paid for, isn't it?'

'Well, yes. But—'

'But they won't really *push* things.'

'I – I didn't know. I thought—'

'Why *should* they?'

'Well – y'know – you know about these things.'

'Of course. I mean, why should they put themselves out trying to find the murderer of a wicked person like Jimmy Doyle? He killed Mrs Sutcliffe. He deserved all he got.'

That was Joyce Frome's contribution to the inquiry.

57

Gossip. Guesswork. Opinions she should have kept to herself, but didn't.

Not too long after the conversation Joyce Frome's listener arrived home and repeated the gist of the conversation to a startled husband. The husband was a lay dignitary at Pullbury parish church. Later that day *he* repeated his remembered version of Joyce Frome's outpourings to the vicar. The vicar was one of that breed of clerics who figure they have a hot and exclusive line to God.

Police wives should keep their mouths shut.

Joyce Frome couldn't!

21

By early afternoon the wind had eased and it had started to rain. Early April rain which still carried the cold sting of a not-so-long-ago winter. It hit the boards of the pier. Soaked the wood and made the surface slippery. It glistened the thick white paint on the pier pavilion's walls and, if you looked over the cast iron of the pier's rails, you could see the heave of the waves pockmarked by the steady drum of droplets hitting the surface.

Lyle had needed back-up. He'd needed one more person in whom he could place absolute trust; one more person with whom he could share his secret.

He'd made a choice. He'd chosen Faber.

Lyle knew all about Faber. Detective Inspector Faber was a music-lover first and, thereafter, he was anything that put food into his stomach and gave him a roof over his head. He wasn't a 'dedicated' copper.

Strangely, that did not make Frank Faber a *bad* police-man. His rank was proof of that. Merely that he worked hard with one object in mind. To earn cash enough to add to an already impressive collection of tapes and records.

The force had better coppers on its payroll. But Faber was the *type* of copper Lyle needed as a back-up.

Faber had a 'trick' brain. It seemed to be made of millions of tiny fish-hooks and, whenever anything mixed with what Faber had between his ears, it stayed. It was caught on the barbs and couldn't work free.

Faber remembered just about *everything*. He saw something, he heard something, he read something . . . and that was it. It was available for instant recall.

The two of them walked towards the end of the pier. They kept their necks shortened into the shelter of turned-up collars and hands deep in the pockets of their macs. They reached the seaward side of the pavilion, and Lyle stepped into the part-shelter of the glass-topped frontage of an as-yet-not-opened pin-table arcade.

'Last seen here,' said Lyle.

Faber nodded.

'There's a disco at the pavilion every Friday night. That's when he was last seen alive.'

'And he's been in the water ever since?'

'The post-mortem should give us a lead in that direction.'

'Currents?' Faber raised himself on to his toes to glance beyond the end of the pier and at the rolling water.

'Not to mean anything,' said Lyle. 'The usual incoming and outgoing tide. No more than that, to my knowledge. We'll check it with the experts.'

'Three weeks?' There was doubt in the question.

'Quite,' agreed Lyle.

Stacked deck-chairs alongside the entrance to the pin-table arcade whipped rainwater at them as an unfastened corner of the tarpaulin covering flapped in the wind.

'The Chief Constable knows?' The question carried concern.

'He knows,' said Lyle.

'I think he'll crawl from under,' said Faber flatly.

'I don't agree.'

'If we come unstuck,' insisted Faber, 'he'll crawl from under.'

'I can't sign a warranty,' said Lyle coldly.

'He's too much to lose,' complained Faber.

'We've *all* too much to lose.'

'You,' observed Faber, 'have a very naïve faith in chief constables.'

Lyle said; '*You* trust *me*.'

'Chief Inspector Lyle,' said Faber, 'I've been hauled in on this thing – remember? *I* trust *nobody*. And, if you doubt that, watch my smoke if things get *too* hairy.'

22

By early afternoon more than sixty officers were working on the Doyle killing. Most of them were pounding pavements, knocking on doors and asking questions they knew couldn't be answered. It was a door-to-door job. Routine. Time-consuming. One way of convincing the citizens that they were getting value for rates and taxes.

It was all top-dressing. Very half-hearted.

'Excuse me, ma'am. It's about the murder of Jimmy Doyle.'

'I hope you're not cadging for a wreath.'

'No, ma'am. Three weeks last Friday – latish on – were you near the pier?'

'No. Why?'

'That's the last time he was seen alive. Near the pier. *On* the pier, actually.'

'Why ask me?'

'Well – y'know – you run one of the pier booths.'

'Not out of season.'

'No, but . . .'

'I see enough of that place *in* season.'

'Yes, ma'am.'

'Actually, I was in Lancaster. Went the Friday, stayed until Sunday night. A weekend with my sister and her husband.'

'I see.'

'Do you want their names and address?'

'It doesn't really matter. It will only mean the Lancaster police visiting *them*. If *you* can't help. . . .'

'Sorry.'

There was no bite to the inquiry. Nobody mourned the passing of James Arnold Simon Doyle. An irritant had been removed from the community – that was about the size of it.

The local television and radio crowd ambled in on the act. Shoulder-cameras were dutifully aimed at bored coppers holding clipboards. Voice-over reporters mouthed clichés about 'the genteel resort of Rogate-on-Sands' and, thereafter, rambled on until the slot was filled, then made for the nearest bar.

The national media didn't want to know.

Doyle hadn't been a pop star. Doyle hadn't been a politician. Doyle hadn't been a famous sportsman. Doyle hadn't been one of the jet set.

Doyle had been a big fat zero, and now Doyle was dead. So who cared?

As one blunt-spoken hotelier put it: 'So Jimmy Doyle won't raise any more hell? Three cheers for whoever stopped his breath.'

23

Muriel Jackson knew what it was like to go crazy. Not a sudden snap – an explosive breakdown – but slowly. Like the gradual tightening of some medieval instrument of torture fixed to the skull.

And yet no real pain. Not even headache. Instead, a numbness. A removal of all feeling and, with it, the ability to think clearly or to concentrate. The refusal of her mind to accept one thought without that thought being swamped by a mass of irrelevancies and half-memories.

Months ago, her doctor had said: 'I think you should see a specialist, Mrs Jackson.'

'A specialist?'

'Somebody who can help you.'

'*You* can help me.'

'Not as much as I'd like.'

'You're a doctor.'

'I'm only a general practitioner. You need somebody with a wider knowledge of this problem.'

'A psychiatrist?' The question hadn't been too far short of an angry accusation.

'Well – yes – a lady psychiatrist, if that's what you want.'

'I don't want *any* psychiatrist.'

'It's good advice, Mrs Jackson.'

'You can't *force* me.'

'No, of course I can't force you, but . . .'

'No psychiatrist.' It had been a flat and final refusal.

'Mrs Jackson, I have to tell you that—'

'No psychiatrist,' she'd repeated. 'It's a backlash from

mother's death. The menopause. That's what it is. It's the change of life.'

'No . . . it's not the menopause.' He'd smiled a sad and helpless smile. 'If it was that, we'd have you back to normal in no time.'

That, of course, had been months ago. Before the black imp *really* dug its claws into her back.

The idea of having a glorified witchdoctor prod and probe into what was happening inside her brain still terrified her. Nevertheless, she'd continued to refuse specialised help.

'We'll try Seconal.' The doctor's remark had carried genuine worry. 'Seconal,' he'd repeated, 'but no more than six a day. Keep it down to four if possible, but no more than six. And, if they don't help, let me know.'

Four a day? Six a day? How many a day? Her inability to concentrate wouldn't allow her to remember.

Orange-coloured capsules of temporary relief. Swallow one then, gradually and for a time, the drowsiness refused the mind the agony of memories. It was a relief – but a relief from what? A relief from life?

When Bob had first seen them he'd been worried.

'Seconal!' He'd turned the tiny bottle in his fingers. 'How many a day?'

'He didn't say,' she'd lied. ' "When necessary." That's all.'

He'd peered at the label and muttered: ' "As directed." That's bloody vague for these things.'

'The doctor says they'll help.'

'Just – y'know – not too many, pet.' The love had still been there in his tone. 'Not too many. They aren't aspirins.'

'I don't know.'

'*I* do. As few as possible, and only one at a time.'

'Of course. I'll be careful.'

'And no booze. One at a time, not too many and no booze.'

'I don't drink,' she'd objected.

'I'm not saying you do, pet. Just – y'know – be careful.'

He'd been hinting at suicide, of course. Policemen knew about these things. Enough Seconal capsules and a stiff drink. That's all it needed. . . .

Not that she would, of course. Although . . .

She dragged her thoughts to the present and to what she was trying to remember. Her fingers fumbled as she replaced the mac on its hanger.

She was sure. *Almost* sure. She couldn't quite recall arranging the daffodils on the grave, but she could *almost* remember throwing the old daffodils on to the compost-heap. She could *almost* remember kneeling in the church and praying.

Her mind stopped short at certainty, because she always knelt and she always said the same prayers.

A prayer for it *not* to have happened. For it all to have been a prolonged nightmare from which they would all awaken.

Always the same prayer – and it was never answered.

As she closed the wardrobe door tears of heartbreak and self-pity spilled from her eyes and rolled down her cheeks.

24

The Regional Forensic Science Lab already had bits and pieces to play with.

The cord had been snipped from the dead man's neck, well away from the knot. The cord *and* the knot might each tell its own tale. The clothes had been removed from Doyle's body. One at a time, each article of clothing had been dropped into its own clinically clean plastic bag. Each bag had been sealed and labelled. The contents of each bag were ready to be microscopically scrutinised. The fibres and the pocket dust would give hours of joy to the scientists and the technicians.

The elderly biologist straightened up from the microscope and said: 'The Green Peace wallahs are right, you know.'

His young assistant waited for some highly technical data.

'This material', muttered the biologist, 'is clogged solid with untreated shit.'

25

Frome had joined Jackson and, together, they watched as the pathologist went about his gruesome business.

Periodically Frome glanced at Jackson, but neither spoke.

It was a standard post-mortem examination. Thorough, but without frills. The cause of death was very obvious. The hyoid bone at the base of the tongue had been snapped by pressure. There was no water in the lungs. Doyle had been dead when he was dumped in the drink.

The pathologist had opened the chest cavity and, without taking his eyes from the few innards left inside and where his blood-soaked fingers searched, he said; 'Reported Missing from Home, I'm told?'

'Three weeks ago,' verified Jackson.

'At a guess, he's been in the water most of the time. Maybe all the time.'

'Oh!' It wasn't really an exclamation. Merely a noise made by Jackson in reply to the pathologist's assessment.

'*Cutis anserina*,' murmured the pathologist. 'Sometimes called "Washerwoman's Hands". Extensive. Not just the soles of the feet and the palms.'

'I'm sorry, I don't. . . .'

'Of course you don't. Why should you?' The pathologist picked up a scalpel and sliced tissue inside the opened corpse. 'The action of water on the thickened epidermis. First sign after about twenty-four hours. As I say, extensive in this case. And the fish have had a few nibbles.'

Frome felt a little sick. The extractor fan hummed, but the stench was still there. He glanced at Jackson, but could read nothing in the detective sergeant's expression.

The door of the mortuary opened and Detective Inspector Faber entered.

The pathologist looked up, recognised the newcomer and said: 'Inspector.'

'Doctor.' Faber nodded a greeting, then spoke to Jackson. 'Sorry to interrupt, Sergeant. Lyle pulled me in to work at street-level. What's under way so far?'

'House-to-house . . . as far as possible. I can't see it amounting to much.' Then, in a flat unemotional voice: 'He seems to have been in the water three weeks.'

'Anything else?' asked Faber.

'This.' The pathologist interrupted his work long enough to point a gory finger. 'He was knocked about a bit before he was strangled. A couple of fractured ribs and bad bruising about the face and trunk. All that happened before he was killed.'

'A fight?' asked Faber innocently.

Jackson said: 'There's no report of anything unusual at the disco. Just the usual noise and a little drunkenness.'

'You've already asked?'

'The Missing from Home inquiry asked.'

'But not *you*? Not you . . . personally?'

'Not yet.'

'Sergeant,' said Faber.

Frome was busy watching Jackson and the pathologist and didn't realise *he* was being spoken to.

'Sergeant Frome,' repeated Faber.

'Oh! Er . . . yes, sir?'

'Are you working in harness with Sergeant Jackson?'

'Yes, sir.' Frome nodded. It was a hurried nod. A shade too eager. 'Chief Inspector Lyle said I'd to—'

'Just to get the picture,' said Faber. 'What comes next?'

'These things to the lab.' Jackson motioned towards the plastic bags containing bits and pieces from inside Doyle.

'Both of you?'

'Well . . . no.' Jackson moved a shoulder.

'How long before you're back asking questions?'

'About . . .' The glance at his wristwatch was quite unnecessary, but it was a natural gesture. 'About an hour. No more than an hour and a half.'

'I'll poach Sergeant Frome from you until you get back,' said Faber. 'We'll backtrack over some of the ground covered by the Missing from Home. This time as a murder inquiry.'

'A good idea,' said Jackson calmly.

'I'll deliver him back at Number One Incident Centre in about an hour and a half.'

26

The reporter's name was Tom Tolby. He knew his name would never be a national by-line. Nor did he want it to be. He'd met a few of the Fleet Street mud-slingers. The journalistic jackals who sniffed out every spicy scandal and didn't give a damn whose hide they nailed to which door.

Terrible men – and some women! Experts at innuendo and behind-the-hand suggestion.

That wasn't for Tom Tolby. He liked his job and he, himself, was liked. He was human enough to *like* being liked. The local law trusted him, and he valued that trust. He didn't screw things up in the name of 'investigative journalism', therefore next time they *again* trusted him.

He was married to a very tranquil lady, had four slightly scatty kids, a mortgage big enough to rupture King Kong and a clapped-out Morris that had a mind of its own. He was a happy man.

He perched on the edge of the chair, opened his notebook but didn't put the ballpoint anywhere near the page.

'Just a few questions,' he smiled. 'If you don't mind.'

Kate Doyle stood on the hearthrug. She wore a stained dressing-gown on top of underclothes, and her bare feet were in ancient slippers. She'd been washing her hair and, as they talked, she rubbed her head with a cheap hand-towel.

'Have the local television and radio people visited you yet?' asked Tolby.

'And why should they want to visit *me*?'

'About Jimmy. About him being murdered.'

'Mr Newspaperman' – her vigorous rubbing seemed to be knotting her hair more than drying it – 'there's no need to worry about me. About what's going to happen to *me*. These television and radio people you're talking about – there'll be nothing they can get from me they can't get from the police.'

'It's – er . . .' Tolby moistened his lips. 'It's what they call "human interest". They'll be interested in what *you* think about your son.'

'And why should that concern them? Why should *that* bring them here?'

'It will,' he assured her.

'And what *should* I think about Jimmy?' She tilted her head in order to rub the nape hairs. 'He's dead. I've lit a candle for him. God knows he'll need it. It'll take more than a candle for *him* to find his way.' She paused, then continued: 'D'you know Cork, Mr Newspaperman?'

'Tolby.'

'What's that?'

'Tolby. My name's Tolby.'

'Is it, now?' She draped the towel across her shoulders and reached for a comb from the mantelpiece. 'I'll ask you, then Mr Tolby. Did you ever go to Cork?'

'No. I can't say I've—'

'It's a darling city, if ever there was one. A *darling* city.' She began to comb her still-damp hair. She tugged and jerked at the knots and, despite its predominance of grey, the hair was strong enough to accept the rough usage. 'It's on the River Lee, y'know. Like here – alongside the sea – but more bonny than here. A lot more bonny. I went there when I was a wee child, a few times. Then when I was a young girl. Lovely times, Mr Tolby. Lovely times, with grand people.'

'Mrs Doyle, I'd like to—'

'I could dance in those days. Light as a feather I was. Dance and frolic with the best of 'em.'

'What I'd like to ask, Mrs Doyle, is—'

'I have a brother there, y'know. In Cork. And Michael – my son Michael – it was his idea. To telephone my brother. My own brother I haven't seen for many a long year. But as nice a man as you'll find on God's good earth. He has a farm, just outside Cork. It's where I'm going. To this farm. To live there a wee while.'

Tolby realised the woman wasn't talking to *him*. She wasn't talking to *anybody*. She was voicing the words of a newly found freedom. She was indulging in memories of a long-ago happiness and daydreaming about a return to that happiness.

69

He closed his notebook and said: 'Mrs Doyle, the police might want to . . .'

'It's a fine farm, Mr Tolby. A fine farm, with fine fields and fine cattle. I'll maybe stay there. Maybe help look after the farm. His wife's a good woman. I've met her, just the once, but we got on fine together. I think she wouldn't mind. . . .'

Tolby eyed the contents of the room. Cheapjack chainstore furniture, polished and cared for as if it was antique.

'Maybe just a holiday, but maybe to stay. Maybe to look around for a wee place of my own. If it doesn't quite work out with my brother, that is. But it will. He's a darling man, so he is. . . .'

The clock on the mantelpiece was a giveaway tin-plate affair. A prize at a fun-fair. But the glass gleamed, and the painted exterior was without a mark. The tick was loud and deliberate; as if the timepiece was aware of the care bestowed on it and, as a result, had become ridiculously proud.

'I'll be going tonight. Michael – my son Michael – he said I'd to telephone. And my brother says I've to come over as soon as I can get. So I'll be travelling down to Liverpool for the ferry to Dublin. . . .'

On the cheap sideboard sat a handful of Mills & Boon paperbacks, neatly stacked and their pages not curled. Their spines were not cracked, yet they left little doubt that they had been read and reread.

Tolby straightened from the chair.

'And he'll be waiting at the station, when I get to Cork. My brother, I mean. He's promised to . . .' She stopped speaking, then asked: 'Have you got what you came for, then, Mr Tolby?'

'Thank you, Mrs Doyle.'

'What was it? This "human interest" you mentioned?'

'Enough,' smiled Tolby. 'Far more than I expected.'

27

The line between Lyle's office and the Chief Constable's office passed through two switchboards. Sometimes switchboard operators were bored. Sometimes they relieved their boredom by listening to conversations.

Each man chose his words very carefully.

The chief said: 'You have Faber with you, of course?'

'Yes, sir.'

'What we discussed this morning, Chief Inspector. It seems you were right.'

'Unfortunately.'

'Therefore, Faber?'

'Therefore, Faber,' agreed Lyle.

'A very invidious situation, Mr Lyle . . . wouldn't you agree?'

'The best course I can think of, sir.'

'Ah, yes. But very invidious.'

'I'm open to suggestions, Chief Constable.'

What sounded like a gentle chuckle preluded: 'Look behind you, Chief Inspector. I'm still there.'

'I'm counting on it, sir.'

'But not indefinitely.'

'Chief Constable, it isn't easy.'

'Nor at this end. Don't forget that.'

'Quite.'

'The media?'

'We've kept a low profile, sir. We haven't waved any flags.'

'I should hope not.'

'All we need is one break,' sighed Lyle.

'Before midnight, tomorrow.'

'Sir?'

'That's when you'll do what you have to do . . . if you haven't done it before.'

'Sir, I think . . .'

'That's an order, Chief Inspector.'

'Yes, sir,'

Lyle replaced the receiver, knowing the chief was right. Nevertheless, being 'right' was sometimes not one of the brightest feelings to have.

28

William Henry 'Mad Man' Dixon had already been questioned about Doyle's absence from the streets of Rogate-on-Sands but, as Detective Inspector Faber put it, 'This is not a Missing from Home inquiry, my friend. Doyle is now jiving in the big disco in the sky.'

Dixon looked less than the glamour shot at the entrance to the pier pavilion. The make-up was missing. So were the sequin-spangled jacket and trousers. In their place were a stained T-shirt and jockey shorts. The tattoos on his arms did not add to his beauty. Nor did the greasy and as-yet-uncombed shoulder-length hair.

'I had a heavy night last night,' complained Dixon as he led Faber and Frome up the stairs and into the one-roomed apartment he called 'home'.

'Park it.' Dixon waved a hand at a studio couch which looked as if if had last been tidied two years ago.

Faber remained standing. He murmured: 'I still have *some* respect for my backside.'

Frome accepted the invitation. He lowered himself on to the edge of the couch and looked worried.

'Last seen alive three weeks ago,' said Faber.

'Yeah.'

'At the pier disco.'

'Yeah.'

'At *your* disco.'

'Yeah.' Dixon dutifully wrinkled his forehead. 'That's bad, man. That is bad.'

'Last seen alive by you.'

'Eh?'

'Three weeks last Friday.'

'Yeah, well . . .'

'Sergeant Frome here would like to ask you some questions.'

This time, Frome said, 'Eh?' blinked and looked startled. Faber said: 'Go ahead, Sergeant.'

'Yes – well – er . . .' Frome took a deep breath. 'The last time he was seen alive was at the disco. Is that right?'

'I guess,' said Dixon carefully.

'By – by you?'

'I run the disco. I spin the platters and MC whatever band happens to be visiting.'

'Band?' Faber cocked a cynical eyebrow.

'Yeah. That night it was—'

'I can guess. Two guitars, three chords, a bloody great amplifier and noise on a par with an elephant farting.'

'Hey, man, we get some of the—'

'Answer the sergeant's questions.'

'Yeah, but—'

'You . . .' Frome moistened his lips, then said: 'You were the last person to see Doyle alive.'

'Hey, I can't say that, for sure. I mean—'

'That's what you told the Missing from Home inquiry.'

'Yeah, but that was only *missing*.'

'If . . .' Frome hesitated. 'If you *were* the last person to see him alive, what time would that be?'

73

'Oh, I dunno.' Dixon scratched his matted hair. 'That's hard to say. Maybe midnight. Maybe half-past. Maybe one. I can't be sure.'

'What time do you turn it off?'

'Eh?'

'The disco. What time does it close?'

'Two.' Dixon lowered his hand. For variety he began to scratch his crotch. 'We have till two. Saturday morning. That's why we have it Friday night, see? If we had it Saturday night, we'd have to—'

'I know.' Frome nodded. 'Who was he with?'

'Eh?'

'Doyle,' snapped Faber. 'We're talking about Doyle, friend. Any questions *I* ask – any questions the sergeant asks – lay money on them being questions concerning Doyle, or you . . . unless we specify otherwise.'

'Who was he with?' asked Frome timidly.

'We-ell. . . .' Dixon managed a sheepish grin. 'He was with me . . . actually.'

'With – with *you*?'

'Yeah. Him and the others.'

'The – the others?'

'Yeah. The guys and gals at the disco.'

'No. What I mean is—'

'Did you kill him?' Faber took over, and his first question was a deliberate bouncer.

Dixon opened and closed his mouth, like a goldfish taking ant eggs.

'The question,' said Faber grimly. 'Did *you* kill Doyle?'

'You – you must be joking,' gasped Dixon.

'Do I *look* like a stand-up comic?'

'For Christ's sake!'

'Dixon, take it from me. Nobody makes detective inspector by doing funny turns at smoking concerts.'

'No. For Christ's sake, *no*. I didn't kill the stupid bastard. Why the hell *should* I?'

'Why the hell *shouldn't* you? Nobody loved the sod. Why should you be so different?'

'Hey, look, man . . . you're—'

'The last person to see him alive,' intoned Faber.

'Who?'

'You. That's what you told the Missing from Home crowd.'

'Yeah, well . . . I guess I *was* about the last person to see him alive.'

'The *last* person. That's what your statement claims.'

'OK. OK.'

'And now he's dead.'

'Yeah. I heard. The local radio. . . .'

'Strangled.'

'Yeah. That's what—'

'Did you like him?'

'Eh?'

'Doyle. Did you like him?'

'Yeah. He was – y'know – OK.'

'You liked him?'

'Like I say, he was—'

'You were one of the minority?'

'We-ell – y'know – I wouldn't say *like*.'

'You *dis*liked him?'

'He was a pain, sometimes.'

'Sometimes?'

'He was trouble.'

'On that Friday night? Three weeks ago?'

'Yeah.'

'Trouble? Trouble *then*?'

'Yeah. He was y'know – working up a head.'

'Trouble?'

'It was coming.' Dixon nodded.

The machine-gun rattle of Faber's questions seemed to hypnotise Dixon.

'Trouble?' snapped Faber.

75

'I – I took him outside.'

'And?'

'I – I talked to him.'

'Talked?'

'I – y'know – I have men around.'

'Men?'

'Attendants.'

'Heavies?'

'They – they can handle things . . . if needed.'

'*Were* they needed?'

'No.'

'No?'

'I - I handled things. Personally.'

'Personally?'

'Yeah.'

'*You* handled it?'

'No sweat.'

'By murdering him?'

Dixon's jaw dropped.

'By strangling him?' rasped Faber.

'Hey! What the hell . . . !'

'No need for heavies.'

'Look, I didn't do a—'

'No need for heavies as far as Doyle was concerned.'

'Jesus Christ!'

'No need for heavies . . . ever again.'

The silence stretched itself for all of ten seconds. It was not unlike a piano-wire being strained to breaking-point.

Then Dixon turned towards Frome and stammered: 'Look – look . . . he's trying to . . .'

'Don't turn to him for support,' rasped Faber.

'Somebody.' Dixon's arm waved helplessly. 'For Christ's sake, *somebody*!'

'*I'm* the one who's going to nail you.'

'But – look – you can't *mean*—'

'The hell I can't. Just give me time.'

76

'Jesus, Joseph and Mary!' It was like a breathed panic-stricken prayer.

'Who else?'

'I don't know. Just not *me*.'

'Doyle. Last seen alive by you.'

'Yeah. But—'

'We have a statement. You signed it.'

'Sure, but—'

'Last seen alive by *you*,' repeated Faber.

'Sure.' Sweat was running down Dixon's face. He was scared out of his wits, and made no pretence not to be. 'Sure. Maybe I saw him. . . .'

'Last seen alive by *you*,' said Faber for the third time. Then he added: 'First seen *dead* by you.'

'*No!*'

'It follows.'

'The hell it—'

'It's bloody *obvious*.'

Dixon lowered himself on to a kitchen chair. His skinny legs trembled as they bent. He sat back-to-front and rested his forehead on his arms. His shoulders shook a little.

Frome watched, wide-eyed and breathless.

He whispered: 'Inspector, don't you think . . . ?'

'*I* think', interrupted Faber, 'that this is going to be a very short murder inquiry.'

'I don't believe this.' Dixon rolled his head on his arms as he spoke. 'I just don't *believe* it.'

'Believe it,' said Faber coldly.

'No. I can't . . .'

'When we get round to charging you, you'll believe it. When you're in the dock – when the jury bring in their verdict – when the judge dishes out the sentence – you'll believe it, sonny.'

'No! It's not—'

'Why *did* you kill him?' asked Faber.

'I keep telling you—'

'He was a ratbag of the first order.'

'I keep telling you—'

'He's no loss to this world.'

'For Christ's sake, man—'

'But why did *you* kill him?'

'Oh, my God!'

'An accident, was it?'

'No. It wasn't an—'

'Deliberate?' Faber raised a warning eyebrow. 'Are we round to telling the truth, then?'

'I - I . . .'

Frome breathed: 'Inspector, I think . . .'

'Let's all forget you said you did it deliberately, shall we?'

'I – I didn't . . .'

'Let's go back to the original suggestion that it was an accident.'

'Please!' Dixon raised his head and pushed the word past clenched teeth.

'You didn't *mean* to kill him. We'll accept that, for starters.'

'Oh, my Christ!'

'If you like, we'll tell the court that, from the first, you've insisted it was an accident.'

Tears were running down Dixon's cheeks. Spittle was dribbling from the corner of his mouth. His expression was that of a weak man battered beyond all hope.

He moaned: 'I think . . .'

'Yes?'

'I think I'd better contact a solicitor. Can I? *Please*?'

Faber smiled at Frome. It was a knowing smile, but without any hint of humour. It was a triumphant smile.

He said: 'That, Sergeant, is when you *know*. When a man asks for a solicitor it means he *needs* a solicitor. He's come unstitched. He's in trouble and *knows* he's in trouble.'

From's face was white, and he didn't reply.

'I – I – I . . .'

Dixon's face was running in sweat. He semed unable to speak.

'Do *you* want to make the arrest, Sergeant?' asked Faber.

'No, I . . .' Frome swallowed. 'I'd rather not, sir. Not at the moment.'

'No?' Faber sounded surprised.

'Not – not at the moment, sir.'

'You may be right,' said Faber slowly. 'Just a touch more evidence, perhaps. That, and his admission.' He turned to Dixon and said: 'We'll be back, sonny. Pull yourself together. Get dressed. Try to act like a man for a change. Oh, and let whoever *needs* to know know. The hard part's over. It's out of your system. That's *always* the hard part.'

29

Lyle worried.

Two decades of bobbying and, to show for it, he had a broken marriage, a flash office and the biggest problem of his career. All that, plus the gut feeling that he was about to be squeezed from the thin end of a very painful horn.

The force was changing. The old loyalties were scorned. The damn force had been brainwashed. This force, and every other force in the United Kingdom. Everything and everybody reorganised until all the hell-or-high-water trust necessary for good policing had been washed down the plughole.

These days the chief constable was little more than a glorified 'managing director'. Superintendents and above were 'top management', and inspectors and chief inspectors 'middle management'. More like a chain of grocer's shops than a law-enforcement body. Tidy up the annual balance-sheet. Keep the shareholders – meaning the rate-and tax-payers – happy. Then stand back and wallow in false glory.

Let the mugs do the graft!

The mugs. A handful of dedicated thieftakers, still sold on the old-fashioned idea of cleaning the streets of filth.

The rest were glorified white-collar workers with an eye on the salary and the pension. Not the job. Sod the job! Aim for the fattest salary and the biggest pension and, thereafter, freewheel into middle age.

Lyle was in a sour mood, and knew it. But what the hell else, with this thing round his neck? What the hell else, with modern policing?

More than fifty per cent of the prats in charge of the force – *any* force – had had damn-all street experience. They knew all the theoretical answers but had never been smacked in the teeth by the practical questions. They were like bricklayers who'd read all the literature about house-building but hadn't once soiled their hands on a brick. Yet *they* gave the orders – they made the decisions – *they* asked the impossible without even recognising the impossible.

He strolled to the window and watched the worsening afternoon weather.

It was, he decided, one hell of a situation, but there wasn't much anybody could do about it.

The Chief Constable was playing reluctant long-stop – but for a very limited period. Frank Faber was out on the street, stirring the broth in his own unique way. Everybody else was unknowingly building a hide from which, with luck, a clear shot might be taken of the killer of Jimmy Doyle.

Lyle scowled at the outside weather, and muttered: 'You stupid sod. You stupid, *stupid* sod.'

30

Meanwhile the Poor Bloody Infantry trudged the streets and wished to hell whoever had stiffened Doyle had chosen better weather. They worked in pairs. Usually an older copper with a younger companion. Sometimes uniformed and plain-clothes. Sometimes a sergeant and a low-ranker. Sometimes a man and a woman. The permutations made little sense because, like the start of every murder inquiry, the object wasn't to make sense. The object was to look *busy*.

The older officer introduced himself and did the talking. His buddy took notes.

'Ah, madam. It's this murder inquiry.'

'Oh, yes?'

'The victim. Doyle. We're trying to trace his last known movements.'

'Yes?'

'The pier disco. Friday night, three weeks ago. He was there.'

'I don't see what that has to do with—'

'Your daughter. Deirdre, isn't it?'

'What about Deirdre?'

'Is she at home?'

'No. She's at work.'

'When *will* she be home?'

'Deirdre?'

'She was at the disco, three weeks ago. . . .'

'Oh, no.'

'She might have seen. . . .'

'She most certainly was *not* at the pier disco three weeks

81

ago. Then, or any other night. If you think my daughter would—'

'We have a statement, madam.'

'I don't care *what* you have. Deirdre was where she always is on a Friday night. At her friend's house. They were busy getting ready for the Save the Children charity-stall on the following Saturday.'

'Until after midnight?'

'Until *well* after midnight. She always is. Deirdre and Claire spend *hours* getting things—'

'Claire?'

'Her friend. Claire Hopgood. They—'

'*She* was at the disco, too.'

'Whoever told you that?'

'Claire Hopgood did.'

'*Claire!*'

'Claire. And Deirdre. They were *both* at the disco. We have statements. At various times they both talked with Doyle.'

'That's – that's . . .'

'They visit the pier disco every Friday night, madam. Didn't you know?'

'Her father'll kill her. He will. He'll *kill* her.'

'Fine. Ask him – as a favour – not until we've asked her a few questions.'

31

Police Constable 417 Jan Gul was feeling slightly miffed. A whole morning and the early part of the afternoon traipsing around the seafront hotels gawping through windows wasn't his idea of a red-hot murder hunt. His feet ached, and the weather had worked its way through the light mac and was touching his shoulders and arms with cold damp fingers.

He entered the DHQ building and, instead of making for the stairs and the incident centre, he hurried along corridors, turned a few corners and ended up in the Divisional Records Office.

The Divisional Records Office was a throwback to the horse-and-buggy days of policing. It should have been 'computerised' years ago, but it wasn't. And it wasn't because of Ma Beecham.

Ma Beecham was a civilian clerk, and that, too, was all wrong. Mere civilians weren't granted unlimited access to the tabulated details of those who, in the past, had had their collars grabbed. Previous convictions and the like were strictly police information with damn near a 'For Your Eyes Only' tab.

Unfortunately Ma Beecham had licked the system.

Nobody knew when she'd started work at Rogate-on-Sands DHQ. On what day she'd wandered into the Divisional Records Office and rearranged things. Why the hell she'd been *allowed* to, and which square-brained nit had stood aside and let her *do* it.

The only certainty was that it was *her* filing system and well beyond the limited comprehension of any mere computer programmer.

As one world-weary copper had once remarked: 'When *she* snuffs it we'll have to start from scratch. Every hook in the bloody division will have a clean sheet.'

She greeted Gul with a smile as wide as her middle-aged hips.

'Now, then, luv. I'm just brewing up. Shall I make it two cups?'

'Thanks.' Gul nodded, then said: 'Somebody called LeFage. Max Leo LeFage.'

'That's a funny name.'

'He's a funny man,' grunted Gul.

The whistling kettle shrieked from an alcove, and Ma Beecham said: 'I'll just see to it, then I'll see if I can help you, luv.'

Ten minutes later, as they sipped sweet and scalding tea, she gave a résumé of LeFage's past life, culled from the various cards and indexes only she understood.

'Homosexual, eh? That was before they made it legal. *Bi*sexual, actually. He's been had a couple of times for Indecent Assault. Nasty with it, it seems. Conduct Likely, a couple of times. Unlawful Wounding. He's been lucky to get away with *fines*, according to this lot. Active member of the National Front, no less. You're right, luv. He *is* a funny man.'

'I wonder what he'd think of a man like Doyle?' mused Gul.

'Chalk and cheese, my luv,' she said confidently. 'No doubt about that. Chalk and cheese.'

32

The tide was ebbing. Pools of sea-water had been left at the base of the prom, but for almost half the length of the pier the rippled and flat surfaces of sand stretched north and south.

Frank Faber had a soft spot for holiday towns out of season. They looked so helpless. The skirts of their finery were wet and unwanted. They were, he figured, like little girls dressed up as a bawd, but too shy to do what they were supposed to do. And the rain was the tears of their unhappy innocence.

Faber had sent Frome back to work with Jackson and he was now pushing his way against rain and wind towards the end of the pier and to where carefully stacked deck-chairs were being soaked because tarpaulin hadn't been lashed properly.

Faber knew how council workers went about their business. He knew that the guys in the fancy donkey-jackets were careful not to upset their official masters, because local councillors always included some creep with a petty mind eager to make noise at meetings and committees about trivia.

In mid-September, when those deck-chairs had been stacked away, that tarpaulin had been firmly lashed into place. Nothing surer. Otherwise, when the deck-chairs were found to be weather-damaged at the start of a new season, Councillor X or Alderman Y would kick up a very personal stink.

As he bent into the wind Faber guessed what he would find – and he was right.

33

Number One Incident Centre was losing some of its glitz. Tea-rings stained some of the surfaces, and one absent-minded flatfoot had left a cigarette smouldering and branded his mark on the polish of a desktop.

Lyle was standing, feet wide, staring at a blown-up street-map of the town. A red circle showed the spot where Doyle's body had been washed ashore.

Lyle turned from the map.

An elderly copper seconded into plain-clothes duty for

the inquiry was touching the surface of a new charge of tobacco in the bowl of his pipe.

'Small,' called Lyle.

The man strolled nearer as he drew tobacco smoke into his lungs.

Lyle said: 'You know this place better than most.'

Small nodded.

'The shore, the sea, the tides.'

'I was born here.'

'You do a fair bit of fishing, I'm told.'

'Off the end of the pier.' Small removed the pipe from his mouth. 'Dabs, mainly. Lots of bones, but tasty if they're done right.'

'Three weeks to be washed ashore.' said Lyle pointedly.

'He didn't go *in* here,' said Small.

'Sure?'

'Positive.'

'The end of the pier?'

'No way. He'd have been on the sand within hours.'

'A boat?' suggested Lyle.

'I wouldn't think so.'

'No?'

'It's not a yachting town, sir. Not like some places. No quay.'

'There's the yacht club and marina.'

'They fart around a bit. They don't do much.'

'You know some of them?'

'A few.' Small eyed the stem of his pipe. 'I know the type well enough. They wouldn't touch Doyle and his crowd with a barge-pole. Different worlds.'

'A job for you.' Lyle seemed to reach a decision. 'Check at the yacht club. The activity over the past few weeks. Mainly the tides and currents. Where he *might* have gone in.'

34

LeFage didn't give a damn who'd been murdered. He had more on his mind than such minor trivialities. Somehow, a wog copper had made him look a bit of a prat, and that *was* important. This bleeding nig-nog had adopted a very high-and-mighty attitude. He'd had the blind bloody impudence to criticise one of his betters for having a telescope at his window.

Him! A flaming rozzer – and a coon rozzer at that!

Well, if they wanted to be awkward, he'd oblige. He'd give 'em something to be awkward about. He'd run 'em round till their balls dropped off.

LeFage had a very self-satisfied expression on his face as he lifted the receiver and dialled the number of Rogate-on-Sands DHQ.

35

Jackson and Frome were back together again, and Jackson was firing on all cylinders.

'He was your pal,' he snapped.

'We went out together, sometimes,' fenced Hammond.

' "Sometimes"? Only *sometimes*?'

87

'Not always.'

'Everywhere. Always.' Jackson paused long enough to give the final contradiction subtle meaning. '*Everything*.'

They were at the rear of the rock-making establishment. As a contrast to the weather outside, the atmosphere was heavy with the scent of melted sugar and caramel. The warmth made a faint mist of steam rise from the shoulders of the officers' macs.

Frome said: 'You were with him the night he died.'

'Was I?' Hammond tried to look and sound tough. Instead, he looked and sounded scared.

'Three weeks back. The Friday night.'

'I was with him at the disco. I didn't know he was—'

'Did you leave with him?' Frome knew the answer, but the deception insisted that he ask the question.

'No.'

Hammond didn't know it, but the interview had cost him his job. The proprietor had made that very plain.

He'd said: 'Christ, not the police again.'

'Hammond,' Jackson had said flatly.

'It's always Hammond.'

'It always *is* Hammond.'

The proprietor had allowed his anger to show.

'He's a blasted nuisance. I've warned him, more than once. Damnation, it's not as if he's a good worker, and he's getting this place a bad name with you people. He can't behave himself.'

'He can't behave himself,' Jackson had agreed. 'He never could. He's the sort of clown who never will.'

'Bugger him,' the proprietor had growled. 'We're better without him. Next time you want him, don't come here.'

'Where is he?' Jackson had asked.

'In the back. You'll want to see him alone, of course.'

'Better that way.'

'I'll get the other two on to something else.'

Hammond was already an unemployment statistic, but didn't know it. The questioning had started. Low-key at first, but quickly up the interrogative octaves.

Jackson took over.

'We think you might know who killed him.'

'How the bleedin' hell should *I* know . . . ?'

'Hold it right there!' snapped Jackson. 'Any red-hot slaver from you, boyo, and you won't know whether your arsehole's punched, bored or counter-sunk.' The stiffened forefinger stabbed Hammond's chest. It was painful, because it was meant to be painful. Hammond winced. Jackson said: 'Check that the doors are closed and locked, Jim.'

Hammond looked worried as Frome checked that they were secure from interruption.

Frome returned, and Jackson said: 'Now we *talk*. Your buddy-buddy is dead . . . right?'

Hammond nodded.

'He died three weeks ago. On a Friday night . . . right?'

'If – if you say so.'

'You were with him on that Friday night . . . right?'

Again, Hammond nodded.

'At the pier disco . . . right?'

'Yeah.'

'Who else?'

'Eh?'

'You, Doyle and who else?'

'The usual. Y'know . . . the usual.'

'No.' Jackson's eyes narrowed fractionally. 'We left the generalities when this thing turned into a murder inquiry. We're on to the specifics. I want names. Lots of names. I want names and addresses. Who was with who. Who talked to who. Who danced with who. Who was groping who. What they were wearing. What they were carrying. Whether they were pissed. Whether they were sober. The lot.'

'For Christ's sake! I can't . . .'

'You *can*. You're *going* to. Understand me, Hammond. We have all the time in the world. The rest of *my* life. The rest of *your* life. We have till Doom cracks. But when we leave here I'm going to know *everything* . . . right?'

It was raw red-necked bobbying. Hard and ruthless. Slowly, as he answered the bombardment of questions, Hammond backed away and Jackson followed him. Then Hammond could back away no more. The small of his back touched the edge of a metal-topped table, and real panic touched Hammond's eyes. The hint of a tremble began to edge itself into his voice.

At times in the past Percy 'Boy' Hammond had counted himself something of a tough nut. In the pubs of London's East End he would have been a mild belly-laugh. In the southern district of Leeds he would have been brushed aside as a small annoyance. In the rougher areas of Glasgow he would have been off-handedly dumped in the nearest bin with the other rubbish. But – horses for courses – in Rogate-on-Sands he had had past moments of glory. In his own midden he was one of the larger rats.

But not today. Not with the hatred Jackson brought to a question-and-answer session which seemed to have no end.

'Who killed him?' asked Jackson.

'Eh?'

'Doyle – your bosom pal – who killed him?'

'How the hell do I— ?'

'Not *that* answer.'

'Eh?'

'I've already warned you. Not *that* answer.'

'I dunno.' Desperation touched the words. 'Honest. I don't *know*.'

'Somebody who hated his guts?' suggested Jackson.

'Yeah. I guess.'

90

'Somebody with *reason* to hate his guts?'

'I guess so,' repeated Hammond.

'Enough hatred to strangle him?'

'Yeah. I – I . . .'

'I know. You "guess so".'

'Yeah.'

'Think about it, Hammond.' Jackson's tone resembled the throaty prelude to a big cat's snarl. 'Give it very careful thought.'

Hammond nodded.

'To strangle him, boyo. To take a length of rope and choke the life out of the bastard.'

'Look. I don't know . . .'

'Somebody must have *really* hated him,' rasped Jackson. 'And with good cause.'

'Look, copper, I . . .'

'Something he'd done.' Jackson refused to be interrupted. 'Something he'd walked away from. Something foul. With you, maybe.'

'Hey! Look . . .'

'You did most things together . . . right?'

'I – I . . .'

'Some terrible thing you did together.'

'What the . . . ?'

'Something like the Sutcliffe killing. Something like *that*.'

Frome breathed: 'Easy, Bob. For Christ's sake . . . *easy*.'

Hammond made no pretence at the tough-guy image. Hammond was terrified. He trembled, and the sweat ran in streams down his face. He seemed to be trying to push himself beyond the edge of the metal-topped table.

'In your shoes . . .' Jackson's voice was low and deadly. 'Hammond, in your shoes, I'd worry. I'd watch my back. Every minute of every day. I wouldn't sleep at night. Because it's possible – it's just *possible* – that whoever stiffened your pal might only have done half the job he set out to do. He might still have notions of completing that job. And *we* might not be too damn keen to stop him. I'd worry about that, Hammond. I'd really worry.'

36

Superintendent Robert Crosby counted himself as a paterfamilias figure as far as the policewomen of the division were concerned. A self-appointed Dutch uncle to whom they could run for comfort when things grew rough.

That's what *he* figured!

What he didn't know was that within the privacy of the policewomen's room he was known as 'Old Fingers'. This, because he was a born 'toucher'. He patted, he stroked and he held their elbows in what *he* considered to be fatherly concern.

But, as one outspoken WPC put it: 'He's a kinky old sod. He gets his kicks that way. I only wish to hell he'd keep his hands in his pockets.'

Crosby it was, then, who strolled past the telephone switchboard room, peeped in, saw the WPC on duty and couldn't resist the temptation to perform his kibitzer routine.

'Ah, my dear.'

The WPC jerked slightly at this unexpected interruption of a slightly boring duty.

'Coping, my dear?' Crosby rested a hand lightly on her shoulder as he leaned across to read the incoming telephone messages. 'Nothing you can't handle?'

'No, sir.'

'Good.' Crosby leaned a little farther. 'A triple-niner, I see.'

'Yes, sir. Somebody called LeFage. He claims to have seen a man damaging deck-chairs at the end of the pier.'

'Good. Good.' The nod was ponderous and paternal, and the WPC tightened her lips as the hand resting on her shoulder became slightly more weighty. 'We know what to do, of course?'

'Yes, sir.'

'Which beat?'

'West Two Beat, sir.'

'And the officer covering that beat?'

'Actually, I was thinking about radioing it out to motor patrol. All the—'

'No, my dear.' The hand squeezed ever so gently. 'The beat constable, miss. The general public like to see the *beat* constable. Police cars aren't quite the same thing.'

'There's nobody on duty on West Two at the moment, sir. The murder inquiry, and all that.'

'Nobody!' Crosby somehow injected gentle shock, minor outrage and elderly understanding into the word.

'Not since Constable Gul left the beat to—'

'Constable Gul, dear.' He smiled pontifical forgiveness. 'Give the complaint to Constable Gul. Make sure *he* deals with it.'

'Yes, sir. But—'

'From me.' He patted her shoulder. '*My* instructions.'

'Yes, sir,' sighed the WPC.

Crosby left, and the WPC blew out her cheeks in relief touched with disgust.

Not for the first time, she wondered why all the jerks ended up with the top jobs. Or maybe the top jobs *turned* them into jerks.

On the other hand, maybe they weren't all jerks. Maybe Rogate-on-Sands was just unlucky.

93

37

Faber dropped the length of cord on to the surface of Lyle's desk and, as Lyle picked it up, Faber said: 'That's the stuff used to strangle Doyle.'

'Really.'

'From tarpaulin covering deck-chairs at the end of the pier.' Faber pulled a chair nearer to the desk. 'At the morgue, that's the stuff they cut from the neck. One corner of the tarpaulin was loose. The cord had been cut off. *That's* from another corner.'

Lyle nodded and looked sad.

'There's a weird character called Dixon.' Faber relaxed in the chair. He seemed happy to take the weight from his feet. 'You should know, in case you get a complaint. Dixon. Disc jockey at the disco. Frome was with me, and I leaned very heavily on friend Dixon.'

'Frome was with you?' Lyle's fingers played with the length of cord.

'Frome was sweating marbles.'

'Devious are the ways of policemen,' sighed Lyle.

'Chief Inspector.' Faber changed from smiles to seriousness. 'We're not after some grubby little tea-leaf. We'll have to invent a few new gags to corner this one.'

'Haven't *you* ever wanted to?' asked Lyle gently.

'Often.' Faber nodded. 'Every time some smartarse lawyer pulls a blinder and some hound who should be out of circulation walks free. Every time some fly bastard cocks a snook at us, knowing we haven't evidence enough to slap him inside. You. Me. Every copper worth calling a copper. But that's not part of our brief.'

'Sympathy?' suggested Lyle. 'Is *that* part of our brief?'

'No,' said Faber flatly. 'Nor is trusting chief constables more than possible.'

'He's with us till midnight tomorrow. That's his assurance.'

'Big of him,' sneered Faber.

'I'm growing old, Frank.' Lyle pushed himself from his chair, thrust his hands into the pockets of his trousers and walked to the window. He stared outside and spoke with his back turned to Faber. 'Too old for this job. I used to enjoy it, but not any longer. These days it's too thick with police politics. This whole bloody set-up. This whole bloody force.'

'Because you don't like what your're going to have to do?'

There was a core of mockery in Faber's question.

'Because of that, too,' admitted Lyle heavily. 'These things matter, Frank. They may not matter to you, but they matter to *me*.'

'What, then?' The question was an open challenge.

Lyle stared out of the window. The rain seemed to have eased, but waves of water running down the glass still distorted the view. After a few moments of silence Lyle answered Faber's question in a voice low-pitched and morose.

'We push it to a successful conclusion. If possible, and before midnight. But, as far as *I'm* concerned, without much joy. We accept certain facts and prepare ourselves to live with them.'

'For example?'

'When this thing hits the headlines we'll all be tarred with as much pitch as the tabloids can rake up. There'll be hints that we've thrown him to the wolves in order to distract attention from other things. There'll be—'

'How the hell can anybody make *that* suggestion?'

'Inspector Faber.' Lyle turned to face his colleague. His jaw muscles quivered a little but, having snapped out the first two words, he continued in a more moderate tone. 'The suggestion *will* be made. Too many people hate us, these days, and too many people are grubbing around seeking excuses – real or imaginary – to justify that hatred. "Dixon of Dock Green" was given the last rites years ago. A whole raft of gullible people have swallowed propaganda hawked from every housetop by every anarchistic group under the sun. Too many idiots can't think for themselves.' Gradually the disgust built up and took over. 'Black is now white, Inspector – or haven't you noticed? Decency is a form of weakness. Doyle – by the time they've finished with Doyle – Doyle will be a bloody *hero*. He won't be a piece of useless dog-dirt who once killed a helpless old woman. Oh, no! *That* particular truth will be kept well under wraps. Doyle will be a whiter-than-white citizen of this town who was done to death because we *allowed* it to happen. Who the hell wants the truth, when rubbish can be so much more interesting? Who the hell *cares* about the truth, when the "pigs" can be made to choke in their own trough?'

'Quite a speech,' murmured Faber.

'Don't you believe it?' Lyle glared.

'Oh, yes, I believe it. Every word. Just that it shouldn't make any *difference*.'

'It *doesn't* make any difference.' Lyle's voice steadied. 'Let me tell you something, Inspector Faber. Something else you'd better believe. This damn case has only a limited time to run. At this moment, you and I are sitting astride the proverbial powder-keg. But the chief says midnight tomorrow, and midnight tomorrow it is. And, unless we find a cleaner way, at midnight tomorrow I touch the fuse, blow the whole bloody thing sky-high and let the scavengers pick up the pieces.'

38

It was closing up to three-thirty and, out at Pullbury, the school-crossing guy was leaning against his lollipop signal and wondering when the little horrors would come howling and racing from the school and whether today would be the day one of them would end up under the wheels of a passing vehicle – and where the thump that would leave *him*.

The number of times he'd complained to the headmaster. The number of times he'd explained that, unless they gathered around the skirts of his officially provided white coat, he could not be held responsible for their safe journey across the road. And the headmaster had always promised full co-operation. But some of the little buggers wouldn't be *told*.

The local vicar passed and nodded a greeting. The school-crossing guy sniffed a bad-tempered reply.

And there went another fool, if ever there was one. Parsons! That particular Bible-basher was of the new breed. He had a personality that upset people. He couldn't leave well alone.

Politics from the pulpit. Amateur rock groups instead of the organ. A great 'modernising' of the Church of England.

He was there, shouting and bawling, at every protest meeting. At every anti-establishment march, he was up front making sure God was on the side of the loonies. He wore the cheap badges of every cockle-brained organisation in the district and happily believed whatever bilge its members spouted, even when it cut across the teachings of his own faith.

He was obviously on his way to perform another spot of do-goodery.

'Money for jam,' muttered the school-crossing guy. 'Suffer little children. He wants to have a go at "suffering" this lot.'

39

Police Constable Small was collecting facts about the movement of boats in and out of the Rogate-on-Sands Yacht Club marina. He, and the young copper with him, were taking their time. It was a cushy number and it kept them out of the weather.

'Nothing suspicious?' he verified. 'Nothing at all unusual during the last three weeks?'

'Most of the craft are moored or cradled, this time of the year.' The club member wore a white cable-stitched turtleneck. His face was lined and ruddy; part weather and part booze. 'You can't just "garage" a boat, y'know. When it isn't being used it has to be seen to.'

The young copper had his notebook open on the bar, alongside an untouched bitter lemon. He scribbled the exchange, verbatim, as Small talked to the club member.

'I was thinking fifteen miles out, maybe,' said Small, in order to prolong the stay in the warmth of the clubhouse.

'Fifteen miles out, and he wouldn't end up here.'

'No?'

'Southport. The quicksands, perhaps. Probably somewhere up the Ribble.'

The atmosphere of the clubhouse was as phoney as antique plastic. A ship's wheel was nailed to a planked wall. Nets and lanterns were artistically arranged in various corners, and brightly coloured buoys gave the place an air of pseudo-nautical authenticity.

Constable Small moistened his lips with rum and pep before he spoke.

'Some of them think he might have been pushed from the pier.'

'Stupid.' The club member sipped at *his* rum. His did not have added peppermint.

'That's what I said.'

'He'd have been ashore by the second tide.'

'Therefore, a boat.'

'Not from here.'

'And elsewhere?'

'The lifeboat boys test their inflatable each weekend.'

'It wouldn't be *them*.'

'No. I'm not suggesting.'

'Fishing?' suggested Small.

'I'd have known.' The club member turned and rested the small of his back against the bar. He steadied himself by backing his bent elbows on its surface. Then he spoke with wisdom and experience. 'Y'see, Constable Small, this place – this Rogate-on-Sands – didn't just *happen*.'

'Sorry. I don't follow.'

'The place was found. The town was built. The Edwardians – the Victorians before them – it grew up around the period when high-priced quacks were hawking sea-bathing as a remedy for every ailment under the sun.'

'Ah!'

'The people who built this place knew what they were looking for. A nice firm beach, gently sloping. And a sea without tricky currents. You don't get muck washed up on *this* beach. No spilled oil. Not even seaweed.'

'True.' Small tasted his rum and pep.

'But,' continued the club member, 'out there you *do* have currents. Nothing savage. Nothing too dangerous. Just a gentle continuous nudge that sends everything either

99

north or south of this stretch of coastline. So whatever gets washed ashore here went in north of here. That, or it went in within the last twenty-four hours. Forty-eight at most.

'Your body – the Doyle clown – was dumped in well up the coast. Three weeks makes sure of that. And that, squire, is not just an opinion. It's an oceanographic fact. Nobody can tool around with tides and sea-currents. Nobody! For what it's worth – and if it helps – you're safe starting with that base-line.'

40

Police Constable 417 Gul opened his heart to Detective Inspector Faber, and Faber listened with some interest.

'I've checked his previous convictions,' said Gul. 'He's the sort of twisted clown who *might* be responsible.'

'For murder?' Faber sounded surprised.

'National Front,' explained Gul. 'The old "Hang-'em-and-Flog-'em-Brigade". And he's definitely kinky. If he met up with Doyle, and Doyle started his antics, LeFage might have—'

'A hell of a lot of "ifs" and "mights",' interrupted Faber.

'We have to start *somewhere*,' insisted Gul.

'True.' Faber nodded.

'And with LeFage's past history it *could* be him.'

'It could be *anybody*,' fenced Faber.

'Anybody who keeps a telescope at his window . . .'

'Ah, yes. The telescope.'

The two officers had met in the incident centre. Faber had been entering and Gul had been leaving. Gul had looked annoyed, and Faber had been a sounding-board for that annoyance.

'Look, sir,' Gul had suddenly appealed to the Detective Inspector. 'I'm on this murder inquiry, and now I have to waste time answering a nine-nine-niner from somebody who's seen a man damaging deck-chairs on the pier.'

'Damaging deck-chairs?' Faber had shown immediate interest.

'He has a telescope.'

'Who?'

'LeFage.'

'And who's LeFage?'

'The nine-nine-nine complainant.'

'The witness to the deck-chair damage?'

'Yes, sir.'

'Tell me more.' Faber's interest had grown.

Gul had obliged. More than obliged. He'd also added the details of LeFage's previous brushes with the law. And Faber had patiently listened.

And now Gul was hoisting LeFage up the flagpole and waving him in the breeze as a possible suspect in the murder inquiry.

'He has this high-powered telescope,' repeated Gul.

'I'll go with you, Constable.' Faber seemed to reach a firm decision. 'We'll give this telescopic enthusiast a quick going-over. Check just what the hell he *has* seen . . . and when.'

41

In theatrical parlance, it was a turkey, guyed up as a smash hit.

Like every other manhunt, the orchestration called for an opening chorus. Therefore, assorted yucks pounded the pavements carrying clipboards. They answered questions, knowing damn well they'd get very few answers. They weren't the high-kickers. They wore size-tens instead of stilettos. It mattered not. Their curtain-up number served the same purpose. To get the show under way. The audience had to be softened up.

The stars were having a last check of their lines, but it wasn't easy. The emphasis kept changing. Even the dialogue wasn't the same from one hour to the next.

The enthusiastic detective inspector sniffed and said: 'Who the hell are we looking for, anyway?'

The sergeant clerk smiled and said: 'A murderer – what else?'

'Yeah, but *who*?'

'Somebody who didn't like Jimmy Doyle.'

'Sweet Jesus! That opens up the field.'

'A few hundred,' agreed the sergeant clerk.

'Meanwhile?'

'We collect paper.'

That was the way it went. That was the way it *always* went.

But this time it was different. Lyle, Faber, Frome and the chief knew exactly *how* different.

But the chorus line didn't know.

42

It was late afternoon, and still a lousy day. The cloud cover was still ten-tenths, with a dirty off-white threat of rain. The wind whipped across, and the slosh and suck of waves against the quay wall added to the slight difficulty of being heard without half-shouting.

Frome looked across the estuary to where the bungalows at Knott End seemed vaguely ridiculous in the dismal light of the afternoon. The white walls were meant to reflect sunlight but, when sunlight wasn't around, they looked like party hats viewed from behind a hangover.

There was no sun, there was no warmth, there was no gaiety. There was only the dirty-looking sky and the mouth of the Wyre which seemed to concentrate the steady chill from the Irish Sea.

Frome wondered why the hell they'd driven almost thirty miles along the coast and ended up at Fleetwood.

Jackson told him.

'He could have gone in here.'

'Eh?' For a moment it didn't register.

'Here,' repeated Jackson. 'It's bloody deep in this part. The Pandora Line runs a three-times-a-day freight trip to and from Dublin.'

'The . . .' Frome moistened his lips.

'The freighters tie up at the wharf,' explained Jackson. 'That's how deep it is. If he went in here, the tides would do the rest.'

'Bob!' Frome's tone had a groaning quality. 'For Christ's sake, Bob.'

'Three weeks.' Frome needn't have spoken, for the effect it had on Jackson. 'That's about right. We'll call at the local nick. Ask if they've had a report of anything. If not, ask 'em to make a few enquiries.'

43

It was quite a day in the life of Kate Doyle.

She was on her way to Liverpool and, as far as she was concerned, British Rail was living up to all its promotional guff.

A young lady had wheeled a trolley down the aisle and offered tea or coffee, *and* sandwiches neatly wrapped in Cellophane. Even paper napkins. Lovely sandwiches, too; fresh and tasty. *And* the tea had been hot and sweet and not served in the old-fashioned thick cups.

All this, and seats as comfortable as armchairs and a handy little Formica-topped table on which to rest your handbag and general bits and bobs. And nice big windows through which you could watch the passing countryside.

This was the life . . . *definitely*!

Kate Doyle, widow. Her husband had died a violent death. Her younger son had just been murdered. Yet, strangely, for the first time in years she was happy.

It was wrong, of course – indeed, it was sinful – but she couldn't help her feelings. Tomorrow – maybe the next day – she'd ask her brother to introduce her to the local priest. Maybe she'd go to Confession and ask for forgiveness. Assuming, of course, that feeling happy required forgiveness.

Meanwhile she felt a twinge of sorrow for the police back in Rogate-on-Sands. Jimmy, of course, had hated them. They in turn had hounded him and, at times, he'd *needed* hounding. For herself, she'd always found the coppers pleasant enough. Even kind – and that was something she hadn't been used to.

When her husband Jimmy – young Jimmy's father – had been killed there'd been an inquest. A nasty drawn-out formality, and the police had insisted she attend. Now there'd be *another* inquest. More quacking and kerfuffling. But she wouldn't be there, this time. Michael would see to things.

Let those who wanted and those who must look solemn, take oaths and tell lies. She was on her way to a personal Paradise and, this time, young Jimmy couldn't stand in her way and forbid. This time nobody dominated her. This time nobody terrified her. *Nobody!*

And after the inquest?

A secret smiled touched her lips. They'd bury him. That, or they'd burn him, *then* bury him. All the hassle, all the form-filling. Simply by buying a railway ticket, she'd passed the palaver on to somebody else.

Without meaning to, she murmured her thoughts aloud.

'They won't leave the bugger on top.'

'I beg your pardon?' The elderly gent sitting opposite her blinked, then stared.

'I'm sorry, sir.' Her smile widened. 'What I was thinking, you see. You wouldn't understand.'

44

A certain amount of gloom and despondency was being spread around Rogate-on-Sands. The house-to-house basics, as always, exposed some of the gingerbread. From the Poor Bloody Infantry's point of view, it was both tiring and boring, but occasionally a tiny nugget of pure gold was unearthed.

'Good afternoon, Officer. What can I do for you?'

'It's about the murder of Jimmy Doyle. We'd like to—'

'Come inside, Officer. Both of you.'

'It's just that a car – we think it was your car – was parked near the pierhead at—'

'Come inside. Come through to the kitchen.'

'Just a quick verification, sir. If it *was* your car—'

'No. no. Not here. Come through to the kitchen. Don't stand here, in the hall.'

'Look, sir, if it *wasn't* your car—'

'Come into the kitchen. It's not the sort of weather to be—'

'Jesus Christ!'

'What?'

'Those two miniatures.'

'The – er . . .'

'Those miniatures. There, on the wall. "Lord Nelson" and "Lady Hamilton".'

'What about . . . ?'

'They're nicked.'

'Really, Officer, I can't see how on earth you can—'

'That's why you want us out of the hall. All this hospitality crap. Into the bloody kitchen.'

'Pleasantries, that's all. Gesture of—'

'Let me tell you something, my little man of pleasant gestures. A year ago – just over a year ago – I flogged myself into the ground looking for those beauties. I hawked coloured photographs of them to all points of the compass.'

'Look, Officer, I can explain. I can—'

'Every damned art dealer and private gallery for miles around. I had dreams about the bloody things. And, all the time, they're sitting here, not five minutes' walk from the station.'

'I – I *bought* them, Officer. I bought them from a man. . . .'

'Good. Pick up the receipt when you collect your coat.'

'Eh?'

'You're going for a walk. You're under arrest.'

45

LeFage was delighted. A detective inspector, no less. That was *really* giving value for money. That *really* showed this nig-nog where the power was.

Gul stood in the background and allowed Faber to set the pace.

'You could see him?' Faber touched the telescope.

'Oh, yes.' LeFage nodded.

'Actually *see* him cutting the rope?'

'Quite clearly.'

Faber bent and squinted through the eye-piece. He adjusted the focus slightly, then straightened.

He said: 'A clear uninterrupted view.'

'Of course,' agreed LeFage. 'And this moron – this raving lunatic—'

'What was he like?' interrupted Faber.

'Just – y'know – just ordinary.'

'Ordinary?'

'About your size. About your build.'

'I'm – er – "ordinary", am I?'

'I'm sorry. I don't mean to sound offensive, but—'

'Go on.'

'For no reason at all, he cut the rope holding the deck-chair cover.'

'No reason?'

'No reason at all.'

'Is that a fact?' Faber's tone was flat and emotionless.

'Senseless vandalism.'

'There's a lot of it about.'

'Destruction for the sake of destruction. No wonder—'

'How was he dressed?'

'A mac. A raincoat.'

'For the weather?'

'I suppose so. Not too differently from the way you're dressed.'

'Did you see his face?'

'No. Not his face.'

'Why not?'

'He had his back to me most of the time.'

'But not *all* the time?'

'He was bent into the wind.'

'A pity,' said Faber solemnly. 'You might have recognised him as somebody you know.'

'I don't have friends like that,' protested LeFage.

'No?' Faber turned to the window. 'You have a damn good view from here.'

'That's why—'

'I could spend hours, watching the world go by – and other things, of course.'

'It's interesting.'

'Sir . . .' Gul spoke for the first time.

'*Very* interesting,' interrupted Faber.

Gul frowned non-understanding, but closed his mouth. He realised that something deep and devious was under way.

Faber continued: 'An uninterrupted view.'

'Quite.'

'The shipping. The pleasure-boats. The windsurfers.'

'And, of course, the pier.' LeFage took the hook without realising it.

'Always something happening on the pier,' agreed Faber.

'Especially in season.'

'The disco?' teased Faber.

'I suppose.' LeFage shrugged.

'Every Friday night?'

'I don't like that sort of music. If you can *call* it music.'

'Nevertheless, lots of activity?'

'Yobbos.'

'Fights? Arguments?'

108

'More often than not.'

'Three weeks ago, for example?'

'The usual set-to . . . as I recall.'

'*Try* to recall,' said Faber gently.

'Is it important?'

'Very important.' Faber smiled. 'Very important indeed.'

'Really?'

'That's why *I'm* here,' said Faber.

'Yes . . . of course.'

'We're sure you can help.'

'Certainly. If at all possible.'

'Doyle – Jimmy Doyle – you didn't know him, of course.'

'Hardly the sort of lout I'd—'

'But you've *heard* of him?'

'Oh, yes. I hear things, but I—'

'Three weeks ago – at the Friday-night disco – Doyle was there . . . as usual.'

The knowing smirk was what Faber had been angling for.

'There was a fight . . . as usual.'

'As usual.' The smirk was repeated.

'Much of a fight?' Faber made it a throwaway question.

'Nothing serious. The way they *always* behave.'

'With Doyle, of course.'

'Of course.'

'But not serious enough to need a call to the police?'

'Oh, no. Not as serious as that.'

'Did you recognise the man Doyle was fighting?'

'No. It was dark, of course. Just the outlines . . . that's all.'

'Doyle and an unknown opponent. Is that it?'

'That's about it, Inspector.'

'Might you be able to recognise the opponent again?'

'Eh?'

'In a line-up? An identification parade? *Might* you? It would help us a lot.'

'I – er – I *might*.'

'Good.' Faber's smile was very man-to-man. He turned

109

to Gul and continued: 'A statement, Constable. That Mr LeFage owns a telescope. That he saw a fight near the disco, three weeks back. That he recognised Doyle as one of the participants. That he thinks he might be able to recognise the man who was fighting with Doyle, on an identification parade. Oh, yes . . . and that he saw somebody vandalising the deck-chairs.'

46

Rogate-on-Sands was no shanty town; no huddle of huts just beyond reach of the sea. Oh, my word, no! Its elders were quite nose-in-the-air about the superiority of the residents of their watering-place. They boasted about its more select 'visitors' during the holiday season and its clamp-down on anything smacking of vulgarity. It was very 'la-de-posh' as the red-nosed comics at less well-regulated resorts along the coast put it. Very 'twenty-Players-and-cut-glass'.

News of the murder had put a temporary stop to all that rubbish!

'Nice people' didn't commit murder. 'Nice people' rarely *got* themselves murdered.

It was all very vexatious.

The late-afternoon edition of the local evening newspaper spread the word to those who couldn't or didn't listen to the local radio. It was front-page stuff and, although the specifics were spread very thinly, the simple fact of murder set the tongues wagging.

Stanley Hammond heard some of the wagging tongues, sent out for a copy of the newspaper and read the report of the murder with compressed lips.

He didn't realise it – and, *had* he realised it, he wouldn't have minded – but Stanley Hammond personified just about everything Rogate-on-Sands held in high regard.

He was the manager of the local NatWest bank. He was a respected member of the local Rotary club. His immediate circle of close friends included solicitors, doctors, accountants, fellow bank managers and some of the more prosperous businessmen of the town. His social life revolved around selected cliques: usually all-male organisations of the you-scratch-my-back-I'll-scratch-yours type.

At work, he lorded it over clerks and tellers, typists and computer operators. At times he was responsible for almost a quarter of a million in banknotes carefully stashed away in the walk-in Chubb at the rear of the bank.

His elder daughter scraped away in the string section of the Hallé Orchestra. His younger daughter was in London training to be an assistant floor manager in BBC Television drama.

His wife took all the right glossies. She was a keen gardener and flower-arranger, and knew all the plants by their Latin names. Her dinner-parties were poems of fastidious correctness, and her sauces and garnishings left her friends wide-eyed with envy. At the round of annual balls given by the better-class charities her tango and her quickstep always brought polite applause.

In short, Stanley Hammond was a well-to-do, well-thought-of member of the community. On a personal level, he was proud of the distaff side of his family.

The private fly in his individual ointment was his son. *He* worked as an unskilled labourer at a small-time rock factory and had been a friend of the murdered Jimmy Doyle.

Hammond's secretary said: 'I understand he was a very unsavoury character.'

'Who?' asked Hammond tartly.

'The youth who was murdered. The Doyle youth.'

'Really?'

111

'I've always held the view that these people deserve all they get.'

'He was . . .' Hammond looked cross as he fished for appropriate words. 'I'm led to believe he was a little on the wild side. Young men sometimes are.'

'I never met him.' The secretary's tone was prim and self-satisfied. 'I wouldn't really know.'

'Nor have *I* ever met him,' said Hammond irritably. 'One hears these things . . . that's all.'

'I'm told he was at the disco thing, on the pier.'

'Was he?'

'The last time he was seen.'

'Indeed?'

'With a group of troublemakers of his own age. Like goes with like, of course. I wouldn't be surprised if one of *them*—'

'We have . . .' Hammond glanced at his wristwatch as he cut in on the secretary's flow. 'We have less than thirty minutes to go before we can call it a day. If you've done all the work for today. . . .'

'Oh, yes. I have, Mr Hammond.'

'I suggest you put the cover on your typewriter, tidy your desk for tomorrow, then retire to the ladies' room and let the rest of us finish *our* work.'

47

Number One Incident Room was showing some of its faults. Computerised policing was not, it seemed, the final breakthrough. One day, when enough people knew how to *use* the bloody things . . .

'*That.*' A detective constable, ancient of days and long

in experience of collar-feeling, stabbed a finger at the cathode-ray tube. 'It's a useless article. Its spiritual home is in a pin-table arcade. It tells us sod-all we don't know already.'

'It has a memory bank.' The solitary operator defended his pet piece of equipment.

'*I* have a memory bank, laddie.' The DC tapped the side of his head. 'It's right here, between my ears, and I don't have to press buttons to get it going.'

'If you press the *right* buttons, it comes up with whatever information you're after.'

'Bloody marvellous! Ask it who killed Doyle.'

'Don't be daft It can't—'

'It's a glorified filing cabinet. That's all it is.'

'It saves space. It—'

'Dammit, we *need* space. You can't detect crime squatting in a cupboard.' The DC waved an all-embracing arm. 'This poky little hole. God Almighty, we haven't room enough to fart in comfort.'

'Look, you can't—'

'I remember the last murder job we had. At the old nick. We used the billiard room. We used the table and the side-forms for the paperwork. Bags of room, and everything was *there*. We could *see* it. It wasn't hidden away inside some fancy goggle-box.'

'Chalk and blackboards!' sneered the computer fanatic.

'Chalk and blackboards,' growled the DC, 'have slapped more men behind bars than any amount of idiot lanterns.'

'It's not a television set.'

'It *looks* like a television set.'

'This thing . . .' The operator was becoming annoyed. 'This thing could have taken the Yorkshire Ripper out of circulation months – *years* - before he'd totted up his final count.'

'The Yorkshire Ripper,' countered the DC, 'was bloody lucky. Too many prize prats horsed around chasing the

113

twisted bastard who sent the fake cassette.' Then, as the clincher: 'That's *exactly* what I mean. Computers. Cassettes. Electronic gadgetry. Expensive crap that gets in the way of *real* bobbying.'

The sergeant clerk joined them and put a stop to a pointless argument.

'It's stopped raining,' he reminded them. Then, to the DC: 'Have an early break. Have a meal, then get back in time to scoop up the workers before they leave home for a pint at the local.'

'And ask them questions?' grumbled the DC.

'What else?'

'What the hell sort of questions are we supposed to ask?'

'You'll think of something.'

'Like "Did you croak Doyle"?'

'That's the question that *has* to be asked, eventually.'

'And, of course, some berk will say "Yes",' said the DC sarcastically.

'He might. He won't if you don't ask him.'

48

The Pullbury vicar was a great one for 'causes', 'freedoms', 'rights' and the like. He wasn't so hot on the more practical aspects of life. On Robin three-wheelers, for example.

The battery was quite flat and, no matter how many times he tried, he couldn't get even the ghost of a cough from the engine.

He muttered, 'Damnation,' and accepted the fact that, however else he was going to get from Pullbury to Rogate-on-Sands, it wasn't going to be in the driving-seat of the Robin.

He hurried to the rear of the vicarage, to where his rather ancient bicycle was propped against the wall. The rear tyre was flat.

He compressed his lips, returned his own bicycle to its resting-place and, instead, grabbed the more modern bicycle his wife used.

As he passed, he opened the rear door of the vicarage and called: I'm borrowing your bicycle, dear.'

From inside, a slightly harassed voice answered: 'No, my dear. I need it. I have to go to . . .'

But, already, the Pullbury vicar was astride the machine, wobbling down the path towards the gate of the vicarage and, like an ecclesiastical Don Quixote, making for a new windmill which had appeared on his horizon.

49

Faber dropped the statement from LeFage on to Lyle's desk.

He said: 'One more tree shaken. Not many apples, I'm afraid.'

He hitched a buttock on to the corner of the desk and waited until Lyle had read the statement.

'It doesn't get us much further,' observed Lyle.

'We're out on a limb, Chief Inspector.' For Faber the tone was very sombre.

Lyle raised a questioning eyebrow.

'Frome's wife,' said Faber. 'Do you know her?'

'I've met her. No more than that.'

'She's mouthy.'

'Oh!'

'She knows too much. The chances are she'll talk.'

'I hope you're wrong.'

'*I* hope I'm wrong, but careful consideration forces me to the conclusion that it's a forlorn hope.'

Lyle rubbed the finger of one hand across his lips, then said: 'The chief gives us until midnight tomorrow.'

'The chief is very magnanimous.'

'You can't expect him to . . .'

'*I* don't give us until midnight tonight.'

'Oh!'

'Decision-time, Chief Inspector Lyle.' Gentle mockery was just under the surface. 'It's time to cop out, or earn our corn.'

'Faber,' said Lyle, heavily, 'I wish . . .'

'Oh, I know what you *wish*, Chief Inspector. You wish you were on annual leave. You wish it had happened somewhere else. In some other division. You wish it *hadn't* happened. But, it *has*. And, it's happened *here*. And you're Jack-the-Lad in charge of the inquiry.'

'Pithily put,' grunted Lyle.

'No . . . not really.' Faber twisted his body slightly in order that he could look directly into Lyle's face. 'You didn't do *me* a favour, Chief Inspector. Sharing your crappy little secret isn't something I'd have wished upon myself. I credit you with doing it for what you thought were the right reasons, but you're wrong. This is where it stops. I don't sleep on it.'

'Suddenly,' sneered Lyle, 'you have a conscience.'

'Do me a favour! Out there . . .' Faber glanced at the window. 'Out there we have a murderer running loose. A smartarse who figures he can beat the system. *Our* system, Lyle. Yours and mine. He figures he has us by the short hairs, and maybe he has – *one* of us.'

'It's not like that, Faber. It's not—'

'You bet your damned life it's not like that,' snapped Faber. He swung himself from the desk and, stiff-armed and with his closed fists resting on the desk surface, he glared at Lyle. 'For reasons beyond my understanding the bastard is being allowed to play footsie with a detective inspector and a detective *chief* inspector. Even with a chief constable. What the hell goes on, Lyle? How come he can shunt rank up some siding? What the hell has he *on* you, Lyle? What sort of hold? What sort of screw can he tighten?'

'Damn it! It's not like that. It's . . .'

'Because he's sod-all on *me*. He doesn't have *me* tucked away in his hip pocket. There isn't some dark and dirty secret he can wave in *my* face and—'

'*That's enough!*' Fury met fury, head-on. 'That,' snarled Lyle, 'is not only enough. It's a bloody sight too much. All right. *All right!*' He took a deep breath and moved his arms in a gesture of helplessness. In a quieter tone, he repeated: 'All right. That's what it might look like. But it's *not* that.'

'In that case, what the hell . . . ?'

'Would you believe "friendship"? Would you believe *that* . . . plus a desire to do a quick hatchet job, with as little hurt as possible?'

'Friendship?'

'It's a word. It has a meaning.'

'With a killer?'

'It's possible.'

'The hell it's possible. You're a—'

'I know what I am, Faber. A gold-plated copper, with a job to do. Something you might not understand, but friendship doesn't come with the town water-supply. You can't twist a valve and turn it off.'

'Therefore?'

'I want him nailed. I'm *paid* to want him nailed. But in a single operation. Quick and painless.'

'In, and nailed,' mused Faber mockingly.

'If it's possible.'

'I don't think it *is* possible. Not the way you want.'

'Because he knows all the angles?'

'Can you think of a better reason?'

'No. But I'm not *saying* it's easy.'

'OK . . . I believe you.' Faber straightened. He pushed his hands into the pockets of his trousers. His accusatory anger had quietened. He said: 'I'm sorry, Chief Inspector. I was wrong. He hasn't got you on something capable of keeping you quiet. But we're paddling very dangerous waters.'

'It's already been mentioned. By the chief.'

'The chief I *don't* trust,' said Faber gently. 'The fall would be too far.'

'You've trusted him until now.'

'I don't know him as well as I know you. With you I might take the risk. With him it's a no-chance bet. If he even *thinks* he's going under, he'll push everybody in sight under the surface first. Chief constables tend to work that way.'

'And so says Detective Inspector Faber,' sighed Lyle. The antagonism had left them. All that remained was a sad understanding. He stood up from the desk and continued: 'Not that I blame you too much. We've been at the point of no return too long, already.'

'We *started* there. This is one we could never win.'

'Maybe.' Lyle picked up the statement. He didn't read it, or even look at it. It was something to do with his hands. He frowned as he forced his concentration, then said: 'Set him up, Inspector.'

'Here? In this office?'

'Yes.'

'What time?'

'You decide. Bait whatever trap you can come up with.'

'Just the three of us?' The thought of the coming confrontation seemed to inject enthusiasm into Faber's tone.

'Set it up,' repeated Lyle. 'It's your interview. I'll play back-up.'

'We'll crack him.'

'Possibly.'

118

'Sir.' There was reluctant respect in Faber's tone. 'It *has* to be done.'

'I know.'

'I – er – I don't know him too well.'

'He won't break easily.'

'What I mean is . . . he's lucky.'

'Lucky?'

'What you said about friendship.'

'Oh!'

'He enjoys more of it than most men.'

'Don't go soft on me, Faber.' Lyle's voice was gruff with emotion. 'Just set the stall out. Start the run-down of the inquiry. Let's not waste any more of the ratepayers' cash.'

50

Frome sat alongside Jackson as they drove south, along the coast. Neither man spoke; Jackson because he seemed to be in a world apart from his companion, Frome because he was worried sick.

As they drove through Blackpool, Frome forced himself to take notice of his surroundings.

He decided he rather liked Blackpool out of season. The illuminations were down. The gimcrack stalls were shuttered. The piers were closed. The promenade was almost deserted. The shows had folded, and the sands were merely playground for a few stray dogs.

The stark shabbiness had a strange beauty.

The trams which, when the crowds were there, lumbered along almost bumper-to-bumper were now spaced at fifteen-minute intervals and almost empty. Even the Pleasure Beach was locked and silent.

His concentration slipped, and his mind flew back to the interview with the disc jockey.

Faber was all set to nail Dixon for this damned murder. Dixon was going to be the patsy – but Dixon didn't do it! That was the way Faber worked. Obviously! Find a sucker, fix him up, then mark the file 'Detected'. Some of the CID animals *did* things that way. They didn't give a damn. Figures - numbers – that's all *they* cared about. And it was going to happen. It was going to *happen!*

Frome fought to bring his thoughts to the immediate present.

Hoteliers and landladies were out. Muffled against the weather, and maybe for the first time in months, they were gazing at the sea which was the reason for their business.

It could be a wild and turbulent sea between November and mid-April. It could slam balks as big as railway sleepers on to the prom; the same sea in which kids happily paddled in summer. But it could flex its muscles, turn nasty and choke the whole promenade with sand and debris. It could stop the traffic, send workmen racing for shelter, hurl itself across prom and roadway, and spend itself against the fronts of hotels and restaurants.

It could be a regular bastard.

Faber, too. *He* could be a regular bastard. Dixon hadn't murdered Doyle. Jesus Christ, he *hadn't*. But the hammer was already between his teeth and, if Faber had his way, he'd be made to suck it.

'Oh, my God!' Frome groaned quietly to himself.

'What's that?' Jackson turned his head in a quick glance.

'Nothing,' said Frome hurriedly. 'Nothing. Nothing at all.'

Jackson returned his concentration to driving, and Frome tried to think of other things.

The sea wasn't rough now. Not today. Today it had a surface like shaved steel. It took the rays of the late-afternoon sun and aimed them at anybody foolish enough to look at the horizon. Every pane of glass was like a mirror. There was light galore – too much light – but no warmth.

It was early April, and Blackpool had settled down to its off-season baleful glare. Like a tired bawd, it had wiped its face clean of cheap make-up and it would refuse to kick its heels again until Easter.

Frome sighed.

Strange . . . Frome liked Blackpool better this way. He wished he could leave the car and walk in the wind. He wished he could forget he was a copper for a few hours. Above all, he wished he hadn't the weight of this awful secret.

51

'Slowly,' said Faber.

The sergeant clerk frowned non-understanding.

'Slowly,' repeated Faber. 'As the men come in, if they've done eight hours or more. One at a time. Not a sudden shut-down.'

'You mean' – the sergeant clerk moistened his lips – 'we *know*?'

They were in a corner of the incident centre. Beyond earshot of the others. They talked in soft conspiratorial tones.

'Just do it, Sergeant,' said Faber gently. 'Don't make it obvious. A skeleton staff here, to keep up appearances. But, as they come in, a quiet word to each in turn.'

'I . . .' The sergeant clerk still looked puzzled. 'I'm sorry, sir. I don't understand.'

'You're not meant to understand.' Faber smiled. 'Just close the book slowly. *Very* slowly. But – y'know – make believe it's still open.'

52

Stanley Hammond's mood was like the gathering of thunder-heads.

'God Almighty!' he stormed. 'A backstreet rock factory. Even *there*. And you can't hold down a job.'

'It was the bleedin' rozzers,' whimpered his son. 'I was sacked because of the rozzers. They come, slinging their weight around, and the gaffer give me the elbow. How's that *my* fault?'

'It's the crowd you knock around with. That's why.' Hammond glared as he tongue-lashed his son. 'That Doyle lout. . . .'

'Jimmy's a good mate. . . .'

'*Was* a good mate. He's no longer around; and I, for one, am not sorry.'

'And what when he gets *me*?' The son was almost in tears.

'What?'

'Whoever killed Jimmy.'

'Don't be ridiculous.'

'He's gonna get *me* next.'

'For heaven's sake don't be childish.'

'The cop said so.'

'Don't be such a young fool.'

'He *said* so. "Watch your back," he said.'

'Of all the . . .'

' "You're next," he said. And they aren't gonna put him away till he *gets* me.'

'Put who away?'

122

'Whoever croaked Jimmy. They aren't gonna lift him till he's snuffed *me* out.'

'Don't be so damned stupid.'

'It's true. He *said* so.'

'Who?'

'Jackson.'

'Detective Sergeant Jackson?'

'Yeah. Then he told the gaffer, and the gaffer sacked me.'

'You lie so easily.'

'I'm not lying.'

'So glibly. You've told so many lies in the past. . . .'

'*I'm not lying.*' Young Hammond was trembling. Something – fear, guilt, anger, something his father had never seen in his son before – was making his whole body shake. He said: 'The sod told me. He as good as *told* me. His mate – that sergeant from Pullbury was with him – he'll tell you. Ask *him*. Jackson warned me. No messing. They aren't gonna lift the bastard who killed Jimmy till he's killed *me*.'

They were in Percy 'Boy' Hammond's bedroom; what he was pleased to call his 'lair'. They were surrounded by the clutter of electronic playthings. Hi-fi speakers hung at angles in the corners of the room. A video-game screen sat on the foot of the divan bed. A portable television set had ben dumped alongside a table on which stood a music centre.

It was a room which gave clear evidence of a pampered child; a son whose own earnings could not have paid for a fraction of what were obviously looked upon as the necessities of life.

And now the son was terrified. His habitual arrogance was missing and this, more than anything, worried his father.

Hammond senior controlled the first surge of anger, and said: 'You've been a disappointment, Percy.'

'I don't see why you should—'

123

'Nevertheless, if you're telling the truth. . . .'

'It's the *truth*.'

'If it *is* . . .'

'Holy shit! It's the *truth*. I *swear*. That plain-clothes pig, Jackson. . . .'

'Are you prepared to repeat the accusation at the police station?'

'Eh?'

'In front of a senior police officer?'

'I keep telling you, for Christ's sake.'

'Quite. But would you tell *him*?'

'How d'you mean?' Percy Hammond's eyes widened.

'You claim . . .' The father sighed. 'You claim to be in fear of your life.'

'It's a fact. Whoever killed Jimmy—'

'The people to be told are the police.'

'Christ Almighty! Isn't it getting *through*?'

'Somebody should be told.'

'That plain-clothes pig, Jackson, as good as—'

'He's only a sergeant.'

'*Only*! He's hard. He knows what goes on.'

'Get ready.' Hammond senior reached a decision. 'Clean yourself up. Try to look a little less like a slob. We'll see if Superintendent Crosby knows what's going on.'

53

It was turning into one of those freak evenings of early spring. After a day soggy with rain and drizzle, the clouds were melting and the sky to the west spewed a changing curtain of colours from a sharp-lined horizon. It was little more than thirty minutes to lighting-up time, but there was a brilliance which the earlier part of the day had lacked.

Lyle had taken time off to use one of the in-house showers installed in the new DHQ. He'd run an electric razor over the hint of stubble to freshen himself up for what was going to be a personal ordeal.

Like the old days of topping. The condemned man had to be clean, bright and healthy before being led to the noose.

Lyle knew that, in a small lifetime of bobbying, this was going to be one of the most distasteful evenings of his career. Maybe one of the most non-productive.

And yet. . . .

With some shame Lyle realised that the adrenalin was flowing. For the first time since the corpse had been washed ashore he felt a sense of excitement. This one wasn't going to be easy. It might not even be possible. This one was no over-ripe lag waiting to be plucked and packed ready for a criminal dock. This one would (in effect) say, 'Prove it,' then sit back and watch the questioners flounder.

As he made his way back to his office, Lyle glanced through a corridor window. He saw the hard-edged brilliance and figured it reflected his own mood. For the moment, the dull rainy period was past. Only clarity remained; the clarity of pure and concentrated interrogation.

54

Liverpool. Scouse Country. Beatle Land. A city with two cathedrals linked by a street called Hope.

Kate Doyle felt she knew the place. Which was ridiculous, because she'd never before been there. But the twin spires, each with a Liver Bird perched at its summit, were as well known as the Tower of London. She'd seen pictures of the romantic stinking Mersey on television dozens of times. She knew that, mile for mile, Liverpool was the birthplace of more stand-up comics than any other place on earth.

Comedians galore, but also some of the most vicious criminals in the country. Funny men and bastards – inner-city squalor and millionaire pop groups – people who cared enough to be heartbroken and people who didn't give a toss as long as *they* slept between silk.

That was Liverpool.

Kate Doyle sensed the 'feel' of the place as she left the train. It didn't worry her. Liverpool was a staging-place on her journey to her brother, and already she seemed to be within touching distance of Ireland.

No more Rogate-on-Sands. No more tears for Jimmy.

She hurried towards the ferry terminal, and a smile of anticipation touched her lips. She was on a sweet journey to her own lost Paradise.

55

Frank Faber joined the Pullbury cleric at the public counter of the DHQ building.

His quick tight smile preluded: 'Vicar . . . I'm a detective inspector.'

'In charge of the murder inquiry?' The cleric's face was flushed; partly from indignation, partly from exertion. The cycle ride had exhausted him a little.

'One of the officers in charge of the inquiry,' Faber fenced.

'In that case, I demand an immediate—'

126

'Not here, Vicar.'

'Look, if you think—'

'I think,' warned Faber gently, 'that you're tending to put rather too much reliance upon that dog-collar. We can talk. We can discuss whatever it is that's upsetting you. What we *can't* do is give you complete freedom to hoist your flag of protest here, where members of the public have free and unrestricted access, and in so doing make a spectacle of yourself.'

'I have a serious complaint to—'

'I know. They rang it through from the desk, here. I'm here to listen.'

'If you think—'

'There's a waiting-room. There – just across the corridor. We'll use that.'

The cleric wasn't arrested. Nothing like that. He was merely grasped firmly by one elbow and guided to the waiting-room. Then, behind a firmly closed door, Faber pointed to a chair and invited the cleric to talk.

The cleric talked, and Faber listened.

A member of the cleric's congregation had been told – by the local police sergeant's wife, no less - that this murder was *not* going to be detected. It was said that, in the opinion of the police, Jimmy Doyle had *deserved* to be murdered, because Jimmy Doyle was himself a murderer. Jimmy Doyle had murdered Mary Sutcliffe, about a year ago. Therefore, the police weren't even going to *try*.

Faber listened, stone-faced and without interrupting, until the cleric had had his say.

Then, very gently, Faber had asked: 'Is that it, then?'

'Is that what?'

'The reason for you being here? The reason for all the puff and palaver out there at the public counter?'

'I'm making an official complaint.'

'Are you?'

'For God's sake . . .'

127

'Let's keep your gaffer out of this. I asked a question. Is that all you have to say?'

'Isn't it *enough*?' The cleric glared.

'Let's get it right.' Faber ticked the points off on his fingers. 'You were told something, by somebody. That somebody heard it from somebody else who, in turn, was told it by her husband.'

The cleric nodded.

'More than a little convoluted . . . wouldn't you say?'

'The husband happens to be the Pullbury police sergeant.'

'And who told *him*?' teased Faber.

'You're dodging the issue.'

'Oh, no. That *is* the issue.'

'I really can't see how . . .'

'How well do you know Mrs Frome?'

'She's . . .' The cleric moved a hand in a vague gesture. 'She's a parishioner.'

'A bit of a gossip.'

'I don't know her well enough to . . .'

'She *is* a gossip,' insisted Faber.

'All right. I'll take your word for that. Nevertheless . . .'

'You're not suggesting that Sergeant Frome is in charge of this murder inquiry, are you?'

'No, of course not. I'm . . .'

'Because, if you *are*, it's rather like holding one of your choirboys up as being a greater authority on your religion than *you* are.'

'Doyle was a murderer,' snapped the cleric.

'Was he?' There was gentle warning in the question.

'Are you saying he wasn't?'

'Does it matter?'

'Eh?'

'If he was – if this wild statement you've just made has any foundation – does it mean anything?' Faber eased the throttles open. 'Does it matter a damn? Unless, of course,

128

you've taken it upon yourself to sit in judgement. To pronounce guilt or innocence. Unless you know something *we* don't know.'

'Look, I'm . . .'

'The only fact that matters is that Doyle is dead, and that Doyle was murdered.'

'That's what *I'm* saying.'

'That Doyle is dead?'

'That he was murdered.'

'And is that why you're here?' snapped Faber contemptuously. 'Is that supposed to be news? Are you seriously under the cock-eyed impression that you're telling us something we don't *know*?'

'Of course. Of course you *know*.' The cleric looked puzzled. A few minutes ago he'd been determined to unearth a forensic whitewash job. Now, in some mysterious way, he'd been turned back upon himself. He'd been made to look foolish; to sound silly and pompous. He stammered: 'Look, Inspector, all I'm saying is . . .'

'You're hawking rumours.'

'Well, I have to . . .'

'Third- and fourth-hand rumours.'

'I – I had reason to believe . . .'

'You're wasting time, Vicar. *My* time. *Police* time. Your ears have flapped, and you've been standing around with your mouth wide open, listening to unadulterated crap. And, because you've nothing better to do – because, once a week, you stand in a pulpit and spout your beliefs without anybody being allowed to call you a liar – you figure you've a hot line to the Almighty. You have the gall to hawk your half-cock yarns in this police station. You interrupt a serious police inquiry. Dammit, it's not too far short of Obstructing the Police.'

'I – I . . .'

'Get back to your church, man. Get back to your Bible class. *Get from under our feet.*'

129

'I didn't . . .'

Faber opened the door of the waiting-room and barked: 'On your way, Vicar. Leave policing to policemen. Concentrate on your own job. Do what *you're* paid to do well enough and – who knows? – eventually coppers might become superfluous.'

56

They were moving towards the outskirts of Rogate-on-Sands, and Police Sergeant James Frome was trying to reach a decision. It was something he wasn't used to. The expression was 'Marking time' and, all his life, Frome had marked time. Not going forward. Not going backward. Just letting things happen, not expecting too much praise but knowing that somebody else would carry the blame if things screwed themselves up.

But not this time, brother!

When his wife, Joyce, had told him the secret she shouldn't have shared, his immediate reaction had been one of disbelief.

Marking time. What you don't like walk away from. If you dislike what you're told, pretend it was never said. Play dumb. Find a quiet little corner, and hide there till things cool off.

He'd done it before. Scores of times. It had enabled him to grow ring-cultured tomatoes in peace and to view policing as a mildly boring job, but with a nice fat pension as compensation for the boredom.

He should have marked time with the shared secret – but he hadn't. He'd passed the secret on to Lyle, and Lyle had decided upon a pattern of action.

Frome glanced sideways at Jackson's profile as the detective sergeant drove the car towards their home base. It was all there, in the features. A strong man. A determined man.

Whereas he (Frome) was a weak man – and now he knew it.

He'd learned so many things in this one day. That he was, indeed, a weak man, playing a part and worrying himself stupid because he had little to gain and everything to lose if he put a foot wrong.

Not for the first time that day, he wished Joyce had kept that damned secret to herself.

57

Police Constable 417 Jan Gul counted himself hard done by and, like most husbands of every colour and creed, he looked upon his wife as a sounding-board against which he could bounce his personal outrage.

'I *found* him,' he complained.

'Not strictly true,' corrected his wife. 'The man with the binoculars saw him first.'

'I was "the officer at the scene".'

'Whatever *that's* supposed to mean.'

'It means it's *my* case.'

'Gully, luv, it's *murder*.'

'That shouldn't alter the rule.'

'Rule? What rule?'

'There, in Standing Orders. It says—'

'For heaven's sake, Gully! It's *murder*.'

'What's the difference?'

'Can't you *see* the difference?'

'No. What's the *difference*?' He refused to be persuaded. 'What's the difference between murder and – and – say, motor manslaughter?'

'How many motor manslaughters have you handled?'

'None. Not yet.' The admission was made grudgingly. 'But I've had more than one drunk-in-charge and a whole heap of motoring offences—'

'Gully, you can't be—'

'—and any one of them could have ended up as motor manslaughter.'

'You're kidding yourself, luv.'

'No.' His jaw jutted slightly. 'A crime's a crime. There's no real difference. It's *my* crime, and they've no right to send me off duty.'

'Because you've been on duty since—'

'Force Standing Orders don't say "except murder". It's there, in black and white. "The officer at the scene" – that's me – shall handle the case or incident. It *says* so. "With the assistance" – that's all, those are the exact words – of any specialised services deemed necessary.'

'You're crazy.' Her impatience began to show itself.

'That's what it—'

'What's the point of CID? What's the point of rank, if the first bobby wearing buttons stays in charge?'

'That's what Force Standing Orders—'

'Force Standing Orders! For God's sake, Gully, see sense. What experience have you? What do you *know*?'

'I know my job.'

'And your job, my luv . . .' She softened her tone. 'Your job – for the moment – is patrolling pavements. *Being* there. Being on tap, in case you're wanted in a hurry. It's not unimportant, Gully. In fact, it's very important. You're what ordinary people mean – what they visualise – when they say "the police". That's your job, until you've had more experience. Until you've had more training.'

'You don't understand.' He unbelted his mac and threw

132

himself into an armchair. His actions were those of a spoiled child. 'They're pushing me out.'

'Gully, don't be—'

'That's what they're doing. They're pushing me out. Deliberately taking the case from me. They're—'

'Who are "they"?'

'Lyle. Faber. All the other white bastards. They say the inquiry's being eased off. That's all balls. That's . . .' He stopped and stared at her. She'd turned her back on him and was looking at herself in the mirror above the mantelpiece. She was touching her cheek with the tips of her fingers. He said: 'What's the matter?'

'Checking,' she said flatly.

'Checking what?'

'The colour.'

'Oh, for God's sake!' He was genuinely shocked. 'I didn't mean *you*. You can't think—'

'You said it.'

'I know. But—'

'You meant it.' She turned, and her expression held a mix of anger and sadness. 'The chip on the shoulder. The ready-made excuse.'

'Pam, I didn't mean—'

'The slick reason, given by every no-good lout whose skin doesn't happen to be white. Not that they're no damn good. Or bone idle. Not that they want everything served up on a plate. Not any of those things, because that would brand them for what they are.'

'Look, I'm not—'

'They can't face the truth, so out comes the old excuse. They're "coloured". They aren't white, and that's a good enough reason for *everything*. Sweet Jesus, Gully, I thought you, of all people . . .'

'I didn't mean it that way,' he pleaded. 'Not *that* way.'

'You meant it,' she said heavily. 'Maybe not now, but when you said it you meant it. You're not in charge of a

133

murder inquiry . . . because you're coloured. Not because you're still only a street-bobby. Not because you wouldn't know where to start. Not for any *real* reason.'

In an empty-excuse tone, he muttered: 'Force Standing Orders say . . .'

'I'm ashamed of you, Gully.' The anger had gone. Only sadness remained. 'I thought you were different. I thought it really *didn't* mean anything.'

'It doesn't,' he pleaded. 'You and me. It doesn't make a bit of—'

'Not just the you-and-me bit. That's easy. Mixed marriages aren't all that uncommon. But I thought you were different. Unique, maybe.'

'I don't know what you mean.'

'Oh, yes, Gully. You know *exactly* what I mean.'

'No.'

'All right.' She took a deep breath. 'I'll spell it out for you. To be called a black so-and-so – even a Sambo – and to accept it, much as we accept it when the Aussies call us Poms. Or the Irish when we call them Micks. Or the Welsh when we call them Taffies. Or the Scots when we call them Mac. That's how different I thought you were . . . and you're not. You only *pretend* to be different.'

'I come from slaves.' Now *he* was getting angry. 'It makes a difference.'

'You,' she said, 'come from good God-fearing folk. Your father was a stevedore, your mother was a seamstress. *My* father was a miner, and my mother worked behind a shop counter. Go back far enough, and I come from serfs – slaves tied to the land – but I haven't been brainwashed into using that as an excuse. I know what I'm capable of. I know what I'm *not* capable of. And my skin has nothing to do with it. Nothing! So don't call any man who's made it to the top a "white bastard". Not unless you're prepared to be called a "black bastard", and not unless you're prepared to include *me* in your dirty talk.'

134

Gul pushed himself from the chair and walked stiff-legged from the room, leaving his wife to weep alone.

58

South of Bedford it is called 'dinner'. Once within sight of the Pennines it starts being called 'tea'. In pseudo-posh hotels and would-be-posh boarding-houses it is called 'high tea'. It can be the main meal of the day or it can be little more than a snack bridging the midday blowout and a fairly hefty supper.

Coppers call it a 'meal break' and, when things become slightly hectic, reduce it to a cup of tea and a quick fag. In a murder inquiry, meal breaks are taken whenever an opportunity presents itself – and this was still a murder inquiry.

59

Jackson had dropped Frome at the DHQ carpark, and Frome had driven his own car back to Pullbury. His was a nice meal. He'd telephoned his wife, before leaving DHQ, and she had it waiting and ready. Grilled trout, from a trout farm nearby. Tiny but succulent new potatoes from his own garden. Spinach, also from his own garden and newly gathered. Home-made chutney.

And, of course, Joyce . . .

Frome chewed his way through a good meal and silently

pondered the problem of this wife of his. It was a problem he had contemplated many times, but he had never reached a satisfactory conclusion.

She was a plump partridge of a woman. He still loved her but couldn't, for the life of him, think why. It wasn't that she was noisy, in the accepted sense of that word. She wasn't 'loud' in any sense. Merely that she was one of nature's tittle-tattles, to whom secrets must never be entrusted. She was a gossip, albeit not a malicious gossip.

Silence – any sort of silence – was to her almost a blasphemy. She talked, but she rarely listened. Whenever anybody spoke to her, she seemed more concerned with what she was going to say next than with what was being said.

At home (as now) the television or the radio – sometimes both – was forever switched on, but she talked over them. Noise. Yackety-yak, from opening her eyes in the morning to closing them in sleep at night.

Frome disliked policing; his wife's continuous talk gave him a vague headache; the only peace he could find was in the garden or the greenhouse. And now, if things went wrong, he could end up behind bars.

But still she talked.

60

The murderer also made his way home for a meal. He called the meal 'tea'. For him, it had been quite a day. Doyle's body being washed ashore had worried him. The quakes had hit him for the first hour or so. Then, gradually, good sense had taken over. A young tearaway like Jimmy Doyle . . . who cared? So he'd been in a fight before he'd been strangled? Doyle had been mighty proud of his reputation as a 'fighting man'.

The murderer was looking forward to the meal.

And why not?

He was as safe as Gibraltar.

61

Faber chose a café.

It was one of a handful of all-the-year-round cafés. It served good plain grub at moderate prices. It was one of the cafés the locals used when they didn't want the hassle of making a quick meal.

The ham was very nice and cut thick enough to taste. The tea was strong and sweet, and served in a sensible-sized beaker. The bread was home-baked and the mustard freshly made.

Fine food . . . but a not-so-fine situation waiting for him back at DHQ.

He was, he decided, in the company of creeps. Lyle, Jackson and Frome. A trio of half-baked prats who, between them, had lumbered *him* with a puzzle not of his own making.

Like Frome, Faber wasn't too keen on his job . . . but for a different reason.

Most of the coppers *he'd* met had the knack of mixing arrogance and deviousness in everything they said or did. They were a breed sociable only with their own kind, and that not too readily. Their enthusiasms were loud, shallow and, in the main, limited. He supposed that when a certain type of man, or woman, was required to wade through filth and degradation for a living some of it rubbed off.

Unfortunately – or so it seemed – too many of those types found their way into the police service, and there was no test or exam ever likely to weed them out before they donned uniform.

Lyle, on the other hand . . .

Faber couldn't pigeonhole Lyle. Lyle was the cat who walked alone, yet he was risking his career for the sake of friendship. And the chances were that the guy at the receiving end of this friendship wasn't even aware that Lyle was his friend.

Lyle could interrogate. None better. But this evening he was stepping down and allowing Faber to take top spot. For the sake of friendship? Or because the forthcoming interview was a dead duck before it even started?

Lyle was the unknown quantity, and that worried Faber.

62

Lyle sent out for food. Crab-paste sandwiches. He wasn't mad about crab and he didn't like paste. The cadet had apologised. 'That's all I could get, sir. The takeaways don't open until later.'

Therefore, crab-paste sandwiches, canteen tea and a case with most of the questions answered but which still fell short of a successful conclusion. It was crazy. To know the killer; to know his name and his whereabouts; to be able to pull him in at the lift of a telephone receiver. To know, within a few hours, when the killing had been committed. To know the method and, thanks to Faber's uncanny powers of observation, know the means and where the killer obtained the means.

To know all these things . . . but to be unable to move with any degree of certainty.

Lyle was an experienced CID man, but this was a situation he'd never before encountered.

Lyle was also a very honest man and, which was far more unusual, he was honest with *himself*. He knew his own weaknesses. He knew his own strengths. He knew what he was doing, and he also knew what other people might *think* he was doing.

It wasn't like the once–upon–a–time years.

Policing, these days, wasn't easy. Sometimes it was damn difficult. Sometimes it was impossible. The boys in uniform had to learn how to police from behind a riot-shield. The boys in plain clothes had to detect crime while pussyfooting around the Civil Liberties crowd. Coppers – plain-clothes and uniformed – were forever playing pig-in-the-middle. Always! They weren't called 'pigs' for nothing.

To some of them – maybe to most of them – it wasn't worth the candle. They opted out and rode the merry-go-round in peace, pending pension-time. Who the hell cared? Keep the damn thing moving, stroll around the nearest corner, let the mad bastards kill each other. All this crap about the Queen's Peace. Half the sods didn't want to *know* about the Queen's Peace, so let 'em get on with it.

Lyle knew all the arguments. At times, he'd been tempted to subscribe to them. It was one of the things wrong with modern policing; the men at root-level had had a gutful and weren't prepared to take much more. Those on the upper rungs didn't know or didn't *want* to know; all *they* worried about was clean noses and making everything look neat and tidy on paper.

Fortunately, in each section – in each division – there was a bare handful of grafters keeping the lid down. Working their nuts off trying to prove that policing still *meant* something.

*Un*fortunately . . .

Lyle chewed crab-paste sandwiches washed down with canteen tea and wished to hell the case hadn't landed in *his* lap.

63

Detective Sergeant Robert Jackson wasn't gagging on crab-paste sandwiches. He'd driven back from Fleetwood and called at his home for a late-afternoon snack.

'There isn't anything.' Muriel Jackson's tone was without life and little more than a whisper.

'An egg. A boiled egg. Something like that.'

'How can you *eat?*'

'Sweetheart, you can't "wish" a person dead, then complain when he *is* dead.'

'I wanted him dead. I didn't want him murdered.'

'You're splitting hairs, Muriel. You wanted him dead . . . that's what he *is*.'

'Oh, my God! Can't you *see?*'

'I can see hypocrisy.' Jackson's tone was heavy with the weight of frustration. He tried to steady his voice as he said: 'You couldn't sleep because of what he'd done. Now he's dead you wish he *wasn't* dead. Pet, you can't have it both ways.'

'Murdered! I didn't want him—'

'*Dead!*' For a moment the accumulated exasperation broke the surface. 'For Christ's sake, Muriel. He's no more dead – no less dead – than if he'd stepped in front of a bus.'

'You don't understand,' she breathed.

'The bastard is dead.' He spoke very deliberately and put much emphasis on the second word. 'Nobody will be arrested for killing him . . . *I'll* see to that. Now, forget Doyle and make me a meal.'

'I – I can't,' she faltered. 'I—'

'I'm your husband,' he interrupted grimly. I've tried to be a good husband. I'm what I've always been. I handle the truth . . . what I believe to be the truth. Not too long ago, and with a little more evidence, Doyle would have dangled from a rope-end. It's what he deserved. You'd have *liked* that.'

'No! That's not true. That's—'

'You're a liar, Muriel. For a year now, you've taken flowers to a grave with a death-wish in your heart. You've wanted Doyle dead. You've—'

'Not killed. Not *murdered*.'

'For God's sake!' Tiny muscles around Jackson's mouth quivered. His fists clenched and unclenched as he fought to control himself. At last he breathed: 'Muriel . . . leave it. Don't! No more. Just – y'know – an egg, that's all. Just a boiled egg, before I go back on duty.'

'No. No! *No!*' Her voice raised itself to a scream as she backed away from him. 'Not for you. Not for *you!*'

64

Nor was the Jackson household the only police family working its way through high drama. To a lesser degree, the Guls were hitting the rough spots.

Pam Gul was quite sure their marriage would never be the same again; that Gul's irrationality, followed by her own outburst, could never be completely forgotten. The marriage would continue, of course, but Gully had suddenly become something she'd never previously noticed. Thanks to his own crazy prejudice, *he'd* suddenly become 'a black man'.

That was the heartbreaking knowledge she forced herself to accept. That Gully himself – the husband she still loved and the husband she'd still fight the world for – had torn aside her own proud principles by exposing, for one stupid angry moment, his own counter-prejudices.

65

The murderer turned a corner in order to reach the National Westminster Bank. Some months previously he'd had a word with the manager, and a mutual agreement had been reached. His was a safe job, with a safe salary. He was a responsible person. He owned his own house. The usual £50 limit could be doubled without risk.

He stopped at the cash dispenser, withdrew £100 and tucked the notes carefully into his wallet, then continued walking towards his home.

In the drive, he climbed into his car and reversed into the road. He checked that the tank was almost full, then drove slowly towards the coast.

66

Faber said: 'We need the Sutcliffe file. Not too obvious, but where he'll notice it.'

Lyle glanced at his watch, as if impatient to get things under way.

'We'll have him,' said Faber.

'You have faith, Inspector,' sighed Lyle. 'Far more faith than *I* have.'

'We'll break him.' Faber sounded certain. 'The right questions. The right technique.'

'He *knows* all the techniques.'

Lyle allowed his eyes to wander around this new office of his. He was already fed up with it. It lacked the intimacy of the old place. It had yet to be 'blooded'.

'Chief Inspector Lyle.' Faber thumbed the light-switch as he spoke, and the neon strips flickered, then sprayed the place with blue-tinged illumination. 'Word has it you're a hot-shot when it comes to easing confessions from guilty people.'

'It has been known.'

'I'm no slouch, either.'

'Another thing I've heard.'

'Therefore, between us . . .' Faber moved a shoulder.

'We are,' said Lyle gruffly, 'going to interview a man who *also* knows the tricks. The soft-guy-hard-guy approach. The triangular set-up. The softly-softly-all-pals-together stunt. The you're-a-damn-liar-even-when-you're-telling-the-truth gag. He can recognise every con before we pull it.'

'Damn and blast it, Lyle!' Faber's exasperation surfaced. 'He's not *that* good.'

'No . . . but maybe *too* good.'

'We almost have him.'

'It's a pretty big "almost".'

'We know he killed Doyle.'

'We *think* he killed Doyle,' corrected Lyle. 'We've been *told* he killed Doyle.'

'The creep LeFage saw it happen.'

'LeFage, in a witness-box?' Lyle's smile was twisted. 'He saw "something" – "somebody" – unrecognised. He thinks they were knocking hell out of another "somebody" – also unrecognised – at the end of the pier.'

'On the Friday night when it happened.'

143

'On just about *every* Friday night.'

'It's – it's . . .' Faber compressed his lips, then moved his hands a little as he reluctantly accepted the size of the task they'd set themselves.

'An innocent man.' Lyle grinned ruefully. 'Oh, sure, *we* know he's guilty . . . or think he is. But a jury might not agree. Who the hell knows which way a jury will jump, unless you have the accused firmly by the short hairs? Now, *he* knows that. He knows the blind bloody impossibility of building a case, unless he breaks. We're tooling around at half-cock, Inspector, and the sooner—'

The door of the office burst open, and Superintendent Crosby exploded into the room.

'Jackson,' he bawled. 'Where the hell's Detective Sergeant Jackson?'

'He's out . . .' began Lyle.

'He's not in this damn building. I've been to the incident centre, but they—'

'He's out on the street, asking—'

'I want him *here*,' snarled Crosby. 'I want him in my office, as soon as possible.'

In a very reasonable tone, Faber said: 'Are we allowed to know why?'

'Threatening behaviour.' Crosby's face was red with outraged fury. 'Hammond's son. Hammond the bank manager – a close friend of mine – threatening his son.'

'Threatening?' Lyle's question had a breathless gentleness.

'Bullying. Losing young Hammond his job. Suggesting – more than suggesting – we're not investigating this Doyle killing.'

'That, sir,' said Faber, evenly, 'is ridiculous.'

'Is it?'

'Quite ridiculous,' added Lyle.

'I'm beginning to wonder what the hell *is* going on,' rasped Crosby.

'A crime inquiry,' said Faber innocently.

Lyle added: 'Specifically, a murder investigation.'

'What the devil sort of— ?'

'You'd like to see Sergeant Jackson?' interrupted Faber.

'In my office,' snapped the furious Crosby. 'And as soon as possible.'

Crosby slammed the door behind him as he left.

'Brother Jackson,' murmured Faber. 'He seems to have a certain knack . . . wouldn't you say?'

'Movement, at last.' Lyle seemed undecided whether to be sad or angry. 'I think we should *all* give Crosby a call.'

'Strange.' A half-smile touched Faber's lips. 'It needed a pompous prat like Crosby to make you see sense.'

67

'You've done it.' Percy 'Boy' Hammond walked the darkening streets alongside his father and almost groaned the words. 'You've *really* done it, this time.'

'If, as you claim,' began Hammond senior, 'this detective sergeant—'

'Can't you *see*?'

'What?'

'They're not going to believe *me*. They're not going to believe *you*.'

'That's a remarkably stupid thing to—'

'Jesus wept! Are you so bloody dumb?'

'Superintendent Crosby – you heard him – he'll get to the bottom of this . . .'

'He'll do sod-all.'

'Of all the outrageous things to say.' The father showed signs of impatience. 'It's his job to—'

'It's his job – it's *every* copper's job – to cover up. He'll tell them – somebody – what you've made me say. Then, some dark night, they'll jump me and do what they did to Jimmy.'

'You watch too much television,' snapped Hammond senior. 'You watch too much violence. All the wrong things. Why should a policeman want to—'

'Because . . .' Percy Hammond closed his mouth.

'Because what?'

'It doesn't matter.'

'It matters to me.'

'Look! Why don't you stay out of this thing? Why don't you stay *out* of it?

'Because, for some impossible reason, you've—'

'The pigs are going to kill me . . . see? Nothing surer. That, or they're going to sit back and watch somebody else kill me.'

'Of all the incredible—'

'They don't give a monkey's toss. Why should they?'

'Will you please stop talking like a cheap—'

'They didn't give a toss about Jimmy. Why should they give a toss about *me*?'

'What the devil *are* you talking about?' Stanley Hammond stopped, grabbed his son by the arm and forced a show-down. He snapped: 'There's something I don't know. Something you haven't—'

'Forget it.'

'The quick half-hearted slap across the face shocked rather than hurt.

Stanley Hammond breathed: 'It's a long time since I thrashed you.'

Percy Hammond remained silent.

'A long time,' repeated the father. 'Too long. But I think I still could, had I a mind. It's what you need. It's what you've needed for a long time. I don't want to, but—'

'You'd better not bloody well try.'

146

'Percy, you're not the hard nut you think you are. You're not even—'

'Hard enough to be with Jimmy Doyle.'

'I don't see what—'

'And *he* was hard enough. He was so sodding hard they had to kill him to keep him down.'

'What *aren't* you telling me?' choked his father.

'Just that.'

'Just what?'

'''Cos nobody can prove it . . . see?'

'Prove *what*?'

'That crazy old Sutcliffe bitch.' The exchange had slipped young Hammond's mouth into overdrive, while his brain was still in third. '*She* bloody soon learned how hard Jimmy was.'

'Sutcliffe? Mrs Mary Sutcliffe? The lady who was— ?'

'*She* bloody soon knew.'

68

They smoked cigarettes and waited. What antagonism there'd been during the day had vanished. They'd both done their best but, from the start, it had been hopeless.

They'd tried to gather evidence enough to force a confession and had collected bits and pieces enough to remove any doubt in their own minds . . . but not enough to convince a jury that there was no 'reasonable doubt'.

'Crosby,' observed Lyle, 'will have kittens on the nearest carpet.'

'It's what he's paid for,' said Faber flatly. 'It's time he had a few more grey hairs.'

'And you?'

'I', said Faber, 'will take tomorrow off.'

'If Crosby doesn't—'

'With or without Crosby's blessing. With or without the blessing of a dozen Crosbys.'

'Ah!'

'Chris Barber has a concert scheduled for tomorrow evening in Southport. I shall be in the audience.'

'He's as good as that?' Lyle seemed genuinely interested.

'If you know jazz – if you appreciate traditional jazz as it should be played – as good as that.'

'I might join you,' mused Lyle.

Faber cocked his head and smiled. For the next few minutes he tried to explain to a non-believer the feeling of a beat that seemed simple but whose simplicity masked an intricacy which had to be sought and found; the nuances which jazzmen fed to those who understood, but which was wasted on ears not both attuned and eager.

'More to it than dance music?' grinned Lyle.

'Dance music!' Faber waved a disgusted hand. 'A gavotte is "dance music". The Morris clowns tool around to "dance music".'

'Point taken.'

'This stuff – the *real* stuff – the stuff Barber pushes out – makes the blood race. It makes the nape hairs tingle. It gets *into* you . . . if you let it.'

'I believe you.' Lyle raised a hand in humorous protest. 'I *believe* you.'

Faber's grin was a little shamefaced. Jazz was one of the main joys of his life, and he knew Lyle could never quite understand. Yet now – thanks to the exchange – there was a companionship which allowed mere disagreement to mean nothing.

He said: 'I would have enjoyed trying to crack it.'

'I would have enjoyed helping you,' sighed Lyle.

'Pity Crosby shoved his foot in the door.'

'Pity,' agreed Lyle.

'Nobody can take a vibe chorus with a German band blasting away in the background.'

'That about sums it up.'

They finished their cigarettes and squashed them into the glass ashtray on Lyle's desk. Lyle glanced at his watch.

'Crosby should be honing his knives,' he murmured.

'He's in for a shock when he finds they're only wooden swords.'

'Let him have his say,' advised Lyle. 'Let him climb to the top of his own little castle.'

'Of course.'

'Then jerk the foundations away and watch him break his bloody neck.'

'Chief Inspector Lyle,' smiled Faber, 'one should not harbour such naughty thoughts about our beloved superintendent.'

69

Detective Sergeant Robert Jackson walked along the promenade, but did not see beauty in the post-sunset sky. He figured he would never see beauty again; never again recognise loveliness or grace.

A year ago there'd been two of them, and Muriel had been happy. She'd had a husband she knew she could trust – a husband she could rely upon – a husband who loved her. She'd had a home of which she was proud.

She'd had a mother, too. She'd loved her mother – maybe a little too much – maybe more than a happily married woman *should* love her mother.

But that had been OK. It had given another dimension to Muriel's happiness.

No kids of course. That had been one of the decisions they'd reached before standing at the altar. No family until later – until they were firmly settled into married life – until a home was ready to welcome maybe one, maybe two children. The plan. Two sensible human beings taking things a step at a time.

Jackson turned towards the sea. He stood with his hands resting on the rails of the prom and stared at the foam-edged waves, but could only see the shambles of his own life.

No kids . . . ever!

At first, no kids *because* . . . Later, no kids because it would have interrupted a comfortable way of life. It would have rocked the boat. Little extras would have had to go.

It had been a good life, and it wouldn't have been possible with the expense and hassle of kids.

On the other hand, *with* kids – even with one – Muriel might have been different. Stronger, perhaps. More able to cope. Less liable – less *able* – to indulge in a prolonged session of self-pity. She might have accepted death more readily because she'd experienced the giving of life.

Front-parlour psychiatry!

Well, maybe . . . maybe psychiatry was only a flash name for honest gumption.

For a year he'd been 'the good and understanding husband'. He hadn't complained. Not even to himself. But there had to *be* a limit, and the limit had been reached.

And now Doyle was dead. His death had been as violent as the death he'd visited upon Mary Sutcliffe. But the old eye-for-an-eye argument hadn't made a scrap of difference.

Jackson felt soul-tired. He pushed himself from the rails and turned his back on the sea.

150

70

'You – you . . .' The father and son faced each other, and the father seemed unable to voice the words. 'Are you – are you telling me . . . ?'

'She was a stupid cow. If she'd handed over the sodding handbag . . .'

'You mean . . . ?'

'All we wanted was a few quid to—'

'We! *We*?' Stanley Hammond's eyes widened. His mouth stayed open for a moment, then he breathed: 'We? You and Doyle? The – murder of Mrs Sutcliffe? Are you – are you . . . ?'

'He hit her,' muttered the son. 'Jimmy hit her. Not me. But she should have—'

'You were there? *You* were there?' The two of you? You were both— ?'

'I keep telling you, *he* hit her.'

Stanley Hammond was not a violent man. He was pompous at times but, with all his faults, he was basically a kind man. He hated extremes in anything.

This being so, when he bunched his fist and hit his son full in the face it was not a crippling blow. It burst the nose and made the blood flow, but little more, because Stanley Hammond didn't know how to deliver a punch. Nevertheless, it sent his son staggering back a few feet, made him stumble from the pavement and ricochet from the side of a passing van before sprawling in the gutter. The fall hurt the son far more than the punch had done.

The van braked to a sudden halt and the angry driver came towards Hammond.

'I saw that,' he stormed. 'Good God, I *saw* that. The

151

youngster wasn't doing a thing, and you hit him.'

'You don't know what you're talking about,' muttered Hammond.

'I know I could have killed the poor bugger. A few yards sooner, and I'd have had no chance. He'd have been under the wheels.'

'That,' said Hammond sadly, 'might not have been a bad thing.'

He watched his son haul himself unsteadily to his feet, then turned and walked away, back towards Rogate-on-Sands Divisional Police Headquarters.

71

Police Sergeant Frome poked his head round the door of Number One Incident Centre.

'Is Jackson back yet?' he asked nobody in particular.

'Shut it!' The sergeant clerk scowled displeasure.

'I only asked. . . .'

'Go home, Jim. It's all over, bar shouting.'

'Oh!'

Frome closed the door and stood, undecided, in the corridor. Something was undoubtedly 'up'. In the few seconds he'd stood at the half-open door he'd caught a feel of the atmosphere. The tension. Something was decidedly askew, and that something *had* to be connected with the murder inquiry. Something big. Something – but of course! – of which he was a part.

His legs suddenly felt weak. He breathed, 'Oh, my God!' and leaned against the wall of the corridor.

Pressed for an admission, Frome would have reluctantly admitted to being a weak man. The post of Pullbury Section

Sergeant was just about his limits. To use his own phrase, he'd 'soldiered on' since first trying the uniform for size. No waves. He'd kept his nose clean. He'd been lucky enough to have had a particularly quiet career.

It happened that way. Often. The sergeant, the inspector, sometimes even the superintendent sat on the throne of the Almighty and took whatever credit happened to be going, while the guys on the beats held various lids in place.

It happened all the time.

But when things went wrong . . .

The realisations came to him with a rush. For a moment, a tidal wave of self-pity threatened to send him scurrying from the building towards some unknown and impossible sanctuary. To run, and keep running, with no thought or idea of destination.

Gradually, he steadied himself. He took a few deep breaths, then turned to make for Lyle's office.

72

Pam knew her husband would be waiting to kiss and make up when she returned home. The knowledge comforted her, *but* . . .

The lamps on top of the goose-neck standards lining the prom seemed to create shadows rather than light at this point of the evening. Rock Walk was where the lovers paraded, but that would be later. For the moment it was deserted. It was private, and she wanted privacy.

After all this time married to him, she *still* hadn't known. She hadn't realised the importance of the colour of his damn skin. To her, it had meant nothing; but, deep down inside, it had meant a lot to him. He was conscious of it, and conscious of the colour of the skin of other policemen.

Gully had turned logic upside down. White men, with years of service and experience, held rank. That was the simple truth. But, to Gully, *white* men held rank . . . full stop. They held rank *because* they were white. Service and experience didn't come into it.

Her life seemed to have quivered a little. It was as if, one day, and given a hard enough push, it might topple. She wasn't quite as sure as she had been.

She thrust her hands deeper into the pockets of the cheap plastic mac she'd slipped on against the cool of the evening. Thoughts and memories mixed in her mind, like garments in a tumble-drier.

There would, of course, be forgiveness, and after the forgiveness, a period of great happiness as a strange compensation. This always happened. But *forgetting* . . . that was another thing.

To 'forgive and forget'. It was a glib phrase, but it meant nothing. Nobody could deliberately *forget*. Nobody could consciously remove something from their memory. It stayed and, periodically, it surfaced to rehaunt.

Like . . .

'Man! You won yourself a real nice piece of white meat there.'
The words remained burned in her memory.

Blackpool Pleasure Beach at the height of the season – a day out on one of Gully's weekly rest-days – a bunch of noisy West Indian yobs with too much booze inside them. As they passed one of them slapped Gully on the back, eyed *her* with contemptuous lust and bellowed the words before opening his mouth wide in a gale of lascivious laughter.

'They're drunk. Don't let's make a scene.'

That had been Gully's muttered reaction as he'd hustled her away and into the crowd. That had been all Gully had said and done when a coloured slob had insulted his wife. For one awful moment the impression had been that he'd associated himself with the West Indian.

For almost an hour there'd been silence between them. They'd been like strangers, walking alongside each other in a packed and noisy fun-fair. Ignoring the roller-coasters . . . not seeing the stalls and the try-your-luck booths. Man and wife . . . but strangers.

Later, in the car, she'd tried to talk.

'The West Indian. What he said.'

'Forget it.'

'For God's sake, Gully. It's not like that, is it?'

'He was drunk. It's not important.'

'Look, I just want to—'

'Forget it.'

But she hadn't been able to 'forget it'. She'd never mentioned it since, and Gully seemed to have flushed it from his mind.

But had he? Indeed, *could* he?

She walked, with head lowered, for another hundred yards or so, then turned and walked back towards her home.

She was wise beyond her years. She knew it would end when she entered the house; when Gully smiled that slow gentle smile that stretched from the corners of his mouth to the corners of his eyes.

She knew it would end . . . but she also knew it would *never* end.

73

Frome opened the door of Lyle's office, closed the door, then leaned with his back against the panels. He stared at Lyle, but seemed unaware of Faber.

'I can't go on with it,' he gasped.

Lyle and Faber watched and waited.

'I can't.' The Pullbury sergeant seemed close to hysteria. 'It's no good. I can't . . . I can't go on with it.'

'Where's Jackson?' drawled Faber.

Frome seemed to see Faber for the first time.

'You and Jackson,' said Faber. 'You are working together.'

'Eh?' Frome blinked, licked his lips, then nodded. 'Yes, sir. Bob Jackson. He's – he's . . .'

'Where is he?' asked Lyle.

'I . . .' Again, the tongue moistened the lips. 'He went for a meal. We both went for a meal. After we'd been to Fleetwood.'

'Sit down, Sergeant.' Faber motioned towards a chair. 'Sit down, before you fall down.'

Frome seemed to collapse into a sitting position, as if his strength had failed him. His breathing was quick and shallow.

Very calmly, Faber said: 'Tell us why you've lost your bottle, Frome.'

'Sir?'

'Why the sudden attack of heebie-jeebies?'

'Crosby?' suggested Lyle.

'Sir?' Frome switched his terrified gaze from Lyle, then to Faber.

'Our illustrious and highly revered superintendent,' said Faber. 'Has *he* been whispering priceless words of wisdom in your ear?'

'Sir, I don't know what you're—'

'All right!' Lyle put bite into his tone. 'Pull yourself together, Frome. Tell us what's happened.'

'Sir, somebody's going to be framed,' moaned Frome. 'We're not just going through the motions. I expected that. I was prepared to go along with that. But the blame is being shifted.'

'The blame?' said Faber innocently.

'The blame. The guilt. Like *you*.'

'Me?'

'The – the disco chap. You questioned him, earlier today. A – a suspect, I suppose.'

'A suspect,' agreed Faber.

Frome stared in near-panic, then blurted: 'Mr Faber, sir. You don't seriously think it *was* Dixon, do you?'

'No.' The accompanying smile was tight and without humour.

'Young Hammond?' teased Lyle.

'Sir?'

'Superintendent Crosby has complained. Something about you and Jackson questioning Hammond.'

'We – we interviewed him.'

'And?'

'Bob – Sergeant Jackson – did all the talking.'

'And?'

'Christ!' Frome shuddered slightly. 'He – he almost told Hammond *he* was next.'

'And you?' asked Faber.

'I'm scared, sir.' Naked truth was in the words and the way they were spoken. 'I didn't know how scared – didn't realise how scared – until a few minutes ago.' Then, to Lyle: 'I'm sorry, sir. That's me finished. I'm not – y'know – not deliberately disobeying orders. Just that this thing is getting too hot for me.'

'You', said Lyle gently, 'are letting yourself off the hook. Is that it?'

'Not just that, sir. It's . . .'

'Letting *everybody* off the hook?'

'I hope so, sir.' Frome shook his head in despair. 'I thought I should tell you first . . . that's all.'

Lyle said: 'Later – when we've contacted Jackson – Inspector Faber, Sergeant Jackson and I are going to Superintendent Crosby's office.'

'Oh!'

'I think you should come with us, Sergeant.'

157

'I'd – I'd . . .'

'Don't worry.' Lyle smiled. 'You've done the right thing. You've obeyed orders. The responsibility is mine. The Superintendent will be told *that*, with no qualifications.'

'Thank you, sir.'

'At which point,' murmured Faber, 'we will all stand around and cheer while the Superintendent takes aboard a certain amount of responsibility.'

74

The murderer drove with caution. He wanted no accidents, but knew he was in no mental condition to be behind the wheel of a car.

Earlier this day, when the waves had rolled the body of Doyle on to the beach, it had all seemed so easy. So safe.

A young tearaway, deserving to die, had been killed. The police would go through the usual play-acting formalities, but nobody would dig very deeply. Why should they? Nobody really *cared*.

But not now. Great God Almighty, not *now*!

He gripped the steering-wheel hard as a counter to an attack of the shakes. He forced his mind to think of the future and not of the past.

He tried to visualise Country Limerick and County Kerry; what they might look like in April and what they *would* look like when summer arrived.

75

Superintendent Robert Crosby was rather enjoying himself. It wasn't often a man detected a year-old murder and, at the same time, had a bank manager eating humble pie. It gave Crosby a sense of munificent power well beyond that which he could claim by reason of his rank.

Hammond ended his story as all such stories end. He ran out of both words and excuses. He stared across the desk at Crosby's face and wondered what the next step would be.

'Quite right, of course, Hammond.' Crosby nodded solemn approval. 'I have no doubt that this hasn't been easy for you. 'Not – shall we say? – enjoyable.'

'Not at all enjoyable,' agreed Hammond.

'Nevertheless, necessary.'

'Of course,'

'*Very* necessary.'

'What happens next?' asked Hammond.

'I – er . . .' For a moment, Crosby seemed to be caught off balance. Then he continued: 'I'll arrange for an officer to come round to your place. Chief Inspector Lyle. He can take a detailed statement from *you* – in the presence of your son, of course – then he can bring your son back here for questioning.'

'Arrest him, you mean?'

'A request to accompany the Chief Inspector to the police station.' Crosby waved an airy dismissive hand. 'The demands of procedure . . . no more. A few basic questions to be asked and answered. A breakdown of what happened.'

'I've already told you. He was with Doyle when . . .'

159

'Ah, yes.' Crosby smiled a very knowing smile. 'But let us be realistic, Hammond. The son of a bank manager. The son of an Irish hooligan. Blame must be apportioned very carefully.'

Hammond compressed his lips, but remained silent. He felt shame at the relief brought on by Crosby's unspoken promise.

'Leave it to me, Hammond.' Crosby stood up and moved towards the office door. 'Have the lad ready for later this evening. Oh, and between these walls, have a decent solicitor waiting with him. To guide him. To make sure he doesn't say *too* much.'

76

The murderer didn't like Preston. It tried to out-Manchester Manchester, but only made a fool of itself. Sometimes it made believe it was the county town, but it lacked the quiet dignity of Lancaster. It had a railway station serving all points of the compass, but the railway station was entwined in an impossible one-way system.

There were, however, adequate parking facilities on the station forecourt.

The murderer parked and locked his car. As he walked towards the station he bent, as if to tie a shoe-lace, and dropped car keys and house keys down the grating of a gutter gulley. It was more than a gesture. There was no going back.

He checked the departure times, then left the station and crossed to the supermarket.

At the checkout he exchanged notes for coins.

At a nearby telephone kiosk he piled the coins in three neat stacks, then dialled a number. He fed the first coin into the slot and said: 'Put me through to the incident centre.'

When the sergeant clerk answered, the murderer identified himself, then said: 'Get this call on tape. And don't interrupt. . . .'

77

Stanley Hammond was, for the moment, a changed man. He would have described himself as a broken man, but that would have been an exaggeration. His cosy world of polite inconsequentialities had been shattered – but, in the long term, that was no bad thing.

As he walked home from his conversation with Crosby he reached some firm decisions.

There would (for example) be no solicitor standing alongside his son when the police came to interview. There would be no excuses and there would be no preferential treatment.

He'd sired a son, and the son had grown into a youth capable of murder. Capable, at the very least, of standing around while a helpless old lady was battered to death for a few pounds.

Hammond felt physically sick as he walked, hunch-shouldered and head bent, towards his home. This was the sort of thing decent people read about in newspapers. It wasn't part of middle-class life. It didn't happen to *bank managers*!

78

The murderer replaced the receiver, collected the coins he hadn't used and left the kiosk.

He felt like a man in mid–Atlantic, who could swim but who'd deliberately allowed a lifeboat to disappear over his limited horizon. Not yet drowning, knowing he was in busy shipping lanes, but aware that his survival would require personal strength and more luck than he'd the right to expect.

He returned to the railway station and bought a one-way ticket to Carlisle.

79

The sergeant clerk said: 'I shifted everybody out, sir. The conversation wasn't on speaker but, once it was taped, I thought it best to keep the room locked.'

'A good decision, Sergeant.' Lyle nodded his approval.

Lyle, Faber and Frome were alone with the sergeant clerk in the incident centre. The replay of the taped telephone call had brought a sombre expression to the faces of Lyle and Faber and a sigh of relief from Frome.

'Crosby?' ventured Faber.

'First of all, his home,' said Lyle. 'If possible, he has to be picked up before he gets too far. His wife might know something.'

'She'll tell you,' said Frome.

Lyle nodded, and said: 'You'd better come with us. You know her well enough. She might talk to you more easily than she'll talk to us.'

'Yes, sir.'

'And you.' Lyle spoke to the sergeant clerk. 'Rewind that tape ready for replay. Lock the door after us and nobody – *nobody* – comes in here until we come back.'

'Crosby?' repeated Faber.

'Crosby,' said Lyle grimly, 'gets it handed to him on a plate. Crosby is one of the reasons for all this behind-closed-doors crap. He gets it when I'm ready to *give* it – and, until then, he can sit comfortably and screw himself.'

80

The murderer was playing it by ear. Distance meant time, and time equated with safety. And yet not in a straight line.

He would stay the night in Carlisle and, tomorrow morning, he would take another £100 from a cash dispenser.

Then more train journeys to Stranraer.

In truth, there was little liaison between the English forces and police north of the border. Scotland, therefore, could be a staging-post.

He settled back and gazed through the carriage window. He concentrated upon what might be ahead in an attempt to wipe his mind of memories of the past.

81

The murderer's home was locked. His car wasn't in the garage. Despite the evening darkness, the house showed no lights. They rang the bell, but nobody answered.

'Break in,' said Lyle shortly.

The murderer's wife was in the living room. She was dead and stiffening. Like Doyle, she'd been strangled but, this time, manual strangulation.

'For Christ's sake, *why?*' Frome stared at the contorted face. 'They were so happy.'

'Were they?' Lyle sounded infinitely sad.

'It wasn't make-believe, sir. I knew them too well for that.'

'They *could* have been happy.' Lyle gave a tiny nod of part agreement. 'I think he loved her. He just couldn't *understand* her.'

'She wasn't crazy, sir.'

Faber murmured: 'They rarely are . . . in public.'

'She was ill, sir.' Frome defended the dead woman and her husband. 'She was a little off-balance, following her mother's murder.'

'And *him?*' asked Faber.

Lyle blew out his cheeks, then said: 'Is anybody sane when they do a thing like this?' Then, in a more business-like tone: 'There's a phone in the hall, Inspector. Get some uniformed men here to stand guard. Nobody inside, nothing to be disturbed until we've heard that tape again.'

82

He was still free. The thought boosted his morale but, at the same time, mystified him and even frightened him. Two murders, and still free.

With something of a shock he realised he'd expected to be caught by this time. The odds were too great. The machine he was pitting himself against was too vast and too well oiled.

Nevertheless, he *was* still free.

The train pulled smoothly out of the Lancaster station. Its final destination was Inverness, and he'd toyed with the idea of going all the way. He'd decided against. Carlisle was the next stop, and that was far enough.

The wise thing was to nibble a way to freedom rather than risk one dash.

Carlisle. Then Stranraer. By ferry to Larne, then south. County Armagh and across the border to County Monaghan.

He'd holidayed on that wild west coast of Eire. It was well away from the 'troubles' and offered a thousand hiding-places and no questions asked.

He settled back in his seat and watched his fellow-passengers through the black mirror of the window.

Better not think too far ahead. For God's sake, don't think of the immediate past. Be free . . . be grateful.

83

Crosby's world was fraying at the edges. His opening gambit had, somehow, skidded out of control.

He'd opened proceedings by barking: 'You're late.'

'We're late,' Lyle had agreed mildly.

'Where's Jackson, and what's Frome doing here?'

'Jackson can't come for a very good reason.' Lyle had lowered himself on to one of the chairs facing Crosby, across the desk. Faber had taken the middle chair, and Frome had perched himself on the edge of the chair farthest from Lyle. Lyle had added: 'Sergeant Frome is here at my invitation.'

'Really?'

Lyle had placed the tape-recorder on the carpet alongside his chair.

He said: 'Sergeant Frome can explain *why* Jackson isn't here.'

'Indeed?' Crosby had sounded very self-satisfied as he'd said: 'Before we start, Chief Inspector, you might be interested to know that, within the last hour or so, I've cleared up one of your undetected murders.'

'Mary Sutcliffe?'

Crosby had stared.

'Murders don't come too often,' Lyle had smiled. 'It was an educated guess.'

Almost off-handedly, Faber had murmured: 'Doyle and Hammond, of course.'

'What!'

Crosby had turned to the Detective Inspector, and *that* was the moment when the stitching became undone.

'Doyle and Hammond,' repeated Faber. 'It's why Doyle was strangled. It's why Hammond had the living daylights scared out of him. It's one of the reasons why we're here . . . or had you forgotten?'

'Eh! Oh! Ah!'

'Most of the CID crowd know it was Doyle and Hammond.' Faber deliberately rubbed Crosby's nose in the dirt. 'The report – the final report, before the file was classified as "pending" – left little doubt. Anybody capable of reading between the lines . . .'

'Quite. Quite.' Crosby made a wild grab at the initiative and missed.

'That's why we're here.' Lyle stepped in to reinforce Faber's domination. 'We know who killed Mary Sutcliffe. We even know who killed Doyle. We've known that – *I've* known that – since before the body was washed ashore.'

'*Known?*' The slack-jawed shock made Crosby look faintly ridiculous. '*Known who killed Doyle?*'

166

'Known.' Faber stepped in. 'Like you "know" who killed Mary Sutcliffe. Knowledge, but no *proof*.'

'Now we have verification.' Lyle glanced down at the tape-recorder. 'It still isn't proof. No court would allow it to be used as evidence. But it's enough to crack him . . . once we've arrested him.'

'What – what . . . ?'

'The tape-recording of a telephone call.'

'Oh!'

'That's why Sergeant Frome is here,' said Faber smoothly. 'To certify that it isn't a hoax. If we can possibly avoid it, we don't want another "Yorkshire Ripper" wild-goose chase.'

'Eh? Oh, no. Of course not.'

'Shall we listen?' asked Lyle politely.

'Yes. Of course. Of course.'

Lyle bent down and pressed the 'play' switch.

From the speaker of the recorder a voice said, 'Are you recording this, now?' and, even with the mechanical distortion, the voice was recognisable.

The sergeant clerk's voice said: 'Yes. It's being taped.'

The voice said: 'Right. No interruptions. No questions. Just let me say what I have to say, then take the recording to Chief Inspector Lyle.'

There was a slight pause, as if the speaker was gathering his thoughts, then the recording continued: 'I wish to state that *I* killed James Doyle. I executed him. He, and his friend Percy Hammond, murdered my wife's mother, Mary Sutcliffe.

'The law requires Motive, Means and Opportunity. I'll try to cover all three, but in reverse order.

'Opportunity. Three weeks last Friday. Going up to midnight – I can't be more precise than that – I wanted some lungfuls of fresh air. And to think things out. Personal things. I parked my car at the pierhead and walked to the end of the pier. The weekly disco thing was going full blast. Everything else was closed. I don't know how

167

long I stood at the end of the pier. Five minutes. At least five minutes. I'd decided to go home when I saw Doyle coming from the side-door of the disco.

'He was drunk. "Nasty" drunk. When he spotted me he let go with a string of obscenities. He was looking for trouble. He wanted a fight. I'm not putting that forward as an excuse. I state it as a simple fact. He was after trouble and he came at me with his fists swinging.

'Because he was drunk it wasn't difficult to clip him on the jaw and knock him cold. Then – because of what he'd done – I lost control. I put the boot in.

'I went too far and I panicked. He was a hospital case and, when he came round, he'd have me. *I'd* end up behind bars. I had to kill him to keep him quiet. Personal survival. I hated the bastard for what he'd put me through and I wasn't going to give him the chance to smash me completely.

'Means? Strangulation. I'd lost control and I was trembling. I wasn't sure I could choke him to death with my hands. I found some cord attached to tarpaulin covering some deck-chairs. I cut a length, tied it round his neck and killed him that way. He didn't regain consciousness.

'I pulled him into the shadows of an arcade and waited. Nobody came to look for him. The disco closed and everybody left.

'I thought of tipping him over the pier-end, but it seemed dangerous. It would have located time and place too accurately. It seemed safer to take the body somewhere else. To deeper water. Somewhere where the tide might take it out and it might not come back.

'The truth is, at a time like that you don't think too clearly. You *think* you're thinking things out, but you're not. During the last three weeks I've gone over it. Umpteen times. I was lucky. That's what it boils down to. Luck. I didn't think things out. Not really. No plan. Not premeditated. Nothing like that.

'Anyway . . .

168

'I stayed around till about two o'clock. Nobody saw me. Nobody saw Doyle. Then I dragged him to the pierhead, backed the car to the gates and managed to get him into the boot. There was no traffic about. No pedestrians. Luck, again – nobody saw me – and I drove up the coast to Fleetwood. That would be about three o'clock. I dumped him in from the deep-water jetty, then drove home.

'Motive?

'It's not easy, but I'll try.

'Doyle – along with Hammond – murdered Mary Sutcliffe, my mother-in-law. But that's not the *real* motive. Not the long-term motive.

'How can I put it? I liked her, I respected her, I never said an unkind thing about her or hurt her in any way. She was my wife's mother, therefore I *liked* her. But I didn't *love* her. Not the way I mean that word.

'Muriel, my wife, though . . .

'She loved her mother very much. Maybe too much. I'm not placing blame. Muriel loved me. She was a good wife. I'm not complaining. Just that . . .

'What I'm getting at is that, when Doyle murdered her mother, it drove her over the edge. Not "madhouse" mad. Not that. Just that she couldn't cope. Couldn't handle things. All that love switched to hate. In a way, she hated Doyle – and Hammond – as much as she'd loved her mother.

'That's why. . . .

'The motive, I mean. . . .

'For a year I'd gone through hell. Impossible demands . . . even though she didn't realise it. The grief, I suppose. It had driven her out of her mind. And – and Doyle had been responsible.'

There was a pause and what sounded like a sigh. A deep, shuddering, soul-draining sigh. Then the voice started up again.

'I told Muriel what I'd done. Not to make her part of

169

it. I thought it might help. To know that Doyle had got what he deserved.

'It was wrong. Stupid!

'She was ill, you see. *Very* ill. But she wouldn't go to the experts. Just tranquillisers. Dope, dished out by the local GP. He was doing his best, but it was beyond him.

'Anyway. . . .

'I told her and, for a few minutes, I thought she'd gone completely crazy. Opening her mouth. Trying to scream, but nothing coming out. She seemed to be choking. She was scared witless. I *think* that's what it was. That I'd end up inside and she'd have nobody.

'It took me more than an hour to quieten her. Tranquillisers. Whisky. Jesus Christ, I was scared!

'Anyway. . . .

'That's about it. We managed to put on a show of normality. We even kept a long-standing evening date with Jim Frome and his wife, out at Pullbury. I'd pulled it. Got away with it. That's – that's what I thought. But. . . .

'There's not much else to tell, is there? Just that I'm sorry, Chief Inspector. Sorry for making a fool of you. You deserve more than that.'

84

The empty tape hissed a little until Lyle bent to press the 'stop' switch.

As he straightened, he said: 'That's why Jackson isn't here.'

'You – you . . .' Crosby closed his mouth, swallowed then choked: 'You knew it was Jackson? Before you switched that damn thing on, you *knew* it was . . .'

'*We* knew it was Jackson,' interrupted Faber.

Lyle said: 'Mrs Jackson told Mrs Frome. Mrs Frome told Sergeant Frome. Very rightly, Sergeant Frome notified me. I shared that knowledge with Inspector Faber, earlier today.'

'Why in hell isn't he under arrest?' exploded Crosby. 'Why in hell isn't he locked up in a cell, being . . . ?'

'Why isn't young Hammond under arrest?' snapped Faber. 'Why wasn't Doyle arrested for the Sutcliffe killing?'

'It's – it's . . .' Crosby sought wildly for words. 'Damn it, man, this isn't the same thing. Jackson's a detective sergeant. He isn't some – some . . .'

'It makes a difference, does it?'

'What?'

'Who commits the blasted murder.'

'Superintendent Crosby.' Lyle's tone was both calm and reasonable. 'We lacked proof. It was a gamble. *My* gamble. It didn't come off.'

'Lyle,' stormed Crosby, 'I'll have you for this. I'll have you up in front of the chief, and—'

'He knows.'

'Eh?'

'He knew this morning. I explained the situation to him, and he agreed to give Jackson enough rope.'

'The Chief Constable!'

Lyle nodded.

'Good God!'

'Superintendent Crosby.' Suddenly Lyle sounded very tired.

'Doyle was no great loss. He was a hooligan and – as far as *we're* concerned – a murderer.'

'Jackson killed his wife.' Frome spoke the words in a dead and emotionless voice. 'Christ! I never thought he'd do *that*.'

Crosby switched his startled stare to Frome.

171

'A miscalculation on my part,' said Lyle heavily.

'And on the part of the Chief Constable, of course,' added Faber. 'This job – you wouldn't know much about it, Crosby, but that's part of it . . . taking chances. Calculated risks. And they don't always come off.'

'If – if I'd known about this . . .'

'You'd have run like hell,' snapped Faber. 'You, and your kind . . . you're the *reason* for these risks.'

'Inspector!' Lyle moved a hand in a gesture of silence. He looked at Crosby, and said: 'We've come unstuck, Crosby. *I've* come unstuck. I wanted Jackson to have enough elbow room to make him feel safe. I hoped he'd give himself away. He *has*.' The quick smile was rueful and unhappy. 'But the elbow room I gave him allowed him to kill his wife. When the chips are down, *that's* my fault, too.'

'And that's it?' asked Crosby in a tight voice. 'That's the sum total? You haven't another rabbit tucked up your sleeve somewhere?'

'That's all. It's enough.'

'There's an Express Message out to all districts,' grunted Faber. 'We know who we're after. He'll be in before morning.'

'*Why?*' breathed Frome. 'Why the hell did he kill his wife?'

'Read the newspapers, Sergeant.' Faber's lip curled. 'When this lot gets out every cheapjack reporter will come up with his own reason. Every do-gooder with an axe to grind will scream "cover-up!" because we let one of our own kind—'

'*Faber!*' Lyle found enough residue emotion to put bite into the word. He rasped: 'You've already said it. It's what this damn job's all about. Cleaning up mess on doorsteps . . . and that includes our own. It's the heat-and-kitchen argument. There isn't a copper in the world who can please *everybody*. There isn't a force in the world. We all make our own decisions, and I made mine. You made yours when you agreed to go along with things and give Jackson enough rope. Great! He has now obligingly hanged himself, and that's what we wanted. Not the *way* we wanted it, but that's something we'll have to live with. Now, if everybody will kindly stop airing their after-the-event wisdom – if everybody will cool down on the smartarse remarks – hand me the nails and the hammer. I will personally crucify the bastard . . . and anybody else stupid enough to stand in my way.'

85

Nobody was crucified.

Next morning, the Preston police found his car. The boffins found evidence in the boot. Evidence enough to convict.

But the trail stopped there.

Unless, of course . . .

Should you ever visit Bentry Bay, north-west of Whiddy Island and south-east of Adrigale. There, at the foot of Caha Mountains, you might find a lonely man. He speaks rarely and ekes out an existence via his own tiny plot and doing odd jobs for those wealthier than himself.

He is a sad man, and nothing seems to remove the sadness from his life.

The locals call him 'Jacko' and he is accepted in that gentle way peculiar to the rural Irish. He does no harm, argues with nobody and faults nothing.

He has one peculiarity. When possible, he hides his hands in his pockets. He seems to *hate* his own fingers!